Go ahead and scream.

No one can hear you. You're no longer in the safe world you know.

You've taken a terrifying step . . .

into the darkest corners of your imagination.

You've opened the door to . . .

They Call Me Creature

Copyright © 2001 by Parachute Publishing, L.L.C.

Special thanks to Mr. George Sheanshang

First published in the USA by Avon 2001
First published in Great Britain by Collins 2001
Collins is an imprint of HarperCollins*Publishers* Ltd,
77-85 Fulham Palace Road, Hammersmith, London, W6 8JB

The HarperCollins website address is www.**fire**and**water**.com

1 3 5 7 9 8 6 4 2

ISBN 0 00 710454 5

The author asserts the moral right to be identified
as the author of the work.

Printed and bound in Great Britain by
Omnia Books Limited, Glasgow

the NIGHTMARE room

They Call Me Creature

R.L. STINE

PARACHUTE PRESS

Collins

An imprint of HarperCollinsPublishers

Welcome...

I'm R.L. Stine. Let me introduce you to the newest visitor to The Nightmare Room. That's Laura Atkins, the tall, pretty girl surrounded by animals. Those are strays Laura found in the woods behind her house.

Laura loves the woods and its creatures. It's where she feels most at home. Unfortunately, there's a creature lurking in the woods that Laura will be sorry she met. In fact, there are several creatures hiding among the trees that don't belong there. That don't belong *anywhere*.

Laura's father has been acting strangely. He used to love walking in the woods with her. But now he orders her to stay away. Does he know something that Laura doesn't? Does he know that the path through the woods leads directly to . . . The NIGHTMARE ROOM?

the NIGHTMARE room

They Call Me Creature

Prologue

They call me Creature.

But I'm not. I'm a human being. I'm a person.

I was born human. I lived most of my life as a human. I am still a human.

I act like a person. I think like a person.

I am not a creature!

Yes, sometimes I get urges. I get such powerful cravings.

When the feeling comes over me, I can't help myself. I can't control myself.

I get so hungry. So hungry . . . as if my whole body needs to feed. And feed and feed.

As I prowl the woods, I must kill for food. I must slash and tear and chew. I fill my belly and keep on feeding. I let the warm juices run down my chin.

Afterward, I force myself to look in a mirror. And I cry out in pain, in sorrow. In shame.

Creature . . . you ugly creature. . . .

I wasn't always like this. I didn't always have to hide my face.

Now I live in the shadows. I have no friends. No one I can trust.

I am so lonely.

I am so tempted to talk to someone. So eager to tell my story to someone who will listen.

But I cannot let my guard down. No one must know. No one must ever know what I am.

That's why I force myself to look in the mirror.
I stare at my face and then I remember.
I remember. I remember.
I remember why they call me *Creature*.

"CAW CAW CAW CAW!"

"It's okay, Mr. Crow," I said softly. I finished bandaging the bird and set it down gently in its cage.

"CAWW CAWWW!" It struggled to flutter its broken wing. "Dad, do you think it will heal?"

Dad didn't answer. He turned the page of the magazine he was reading.

"Dad? What do you think?"

He picked up a pencil and circled a sentence on the page.

"Dad?"

"Did you say something, Laura?" My father glanced up and squinted at me through his thick, black-framed glasses.

"Do you think the wing will heal?" I asked again.

"What wing?" Dad returned to the magazine and started scribbling notes in the margin.

I caught the surprise on my friend Ellen's face. She hadn't seen Dad's new faraway personality.

Far away.

That was the best way to describe my father these days. Even when we were in the same room together, he seemed to be someplace else.

Lucky, the big stray cat I'd found in the woods, bumped past me, nearly knocking over the birdcage. He began licking Dad's hand with his long tongue.

Dad jerked his hand away. "Please take the cat out. I'm trying to concentrate." He circled more sentences, pressing so hard, the pencil point broke with a sharp snap.

"Where am I supposed to put him?" I sighed. "I can't use the shed anymore since you're working in there."

Dad stared at the crow and Lucky, as if seeing them for the first time. "Why can't I live in a house, Laura? Why do I have to live in a zoo?"

"You're a vet!" I cried. "You're supposed to love animals—remember?"

Ellen forced a laugh. But I could see she was really embarrassed. She had never seen Dad and me yelling at each other. She hadn't seen Dad since . . . since he changed.

I had stopped inviting my friends over because I never knew what Dad was going to say or do. But Ellen was my best friend, and I missed hanging out with her. So I asked her to come over today. But maybe it was a big mistake.

I picked up the cage in one hand and Lucky in

the other. I took them both down the hall to my room and shut the door.

I swung my camera around my neck. "Come on, Ellen," I said. "Let's get to the woods."

Our house sits on the edge of a quiet country road. Our back lawn is deep and lush and ends at the woods. So I've always considered the woods and the little streams that flow through it part of my backyard.

That's where I feel the happiest. It's so beautiful in the woods, so peaceful and filled with life.

In the mornings before I go to school, I stand in the center of our lawn and stare out at tall, leafy trees that seem to stretch on forever. Then I breathe in the morning scent of fresh pine. I love that smell.

I checked out my camera, making sure I had put in a new film cartridge.

Ellen brushed back her straight, black hair. She loves her hair. She's always pushing it back, pulling it to the side, sweeping her hands through it.

I'm totally jealous of her hair. Mine is long, and red-brown. It's totally unmanageable.

Ellen's eyes flashed. "Are we going into the woods because of your science project? Or because you want to see that boy you met there last week?"

I let out a groan. "Because of my project," I said. "Life isn't only about boys, you know."

"Well, you're the one who was talking about him all morning. 'I wonder if I'll see him again. I wonder

3

where he lives. I wonder if he has a girlfriend. . . .'"
She laughed.

"Okay. Okay." I had to admit it. I had been thinking about Joe a lot since I ran into him by Luker
Pond.

"It's just that boys don't usually notice me," I said.
"And he seemed so nice. And when I told him about
my science project, he seemed really interested."

"Then we have two projects," Ellen stated. "The
science project and the boy project! Let's go."

"We just have to find Georgie," I said.

"You're going into the woods?" Dad frowned at
me. "You need other interests, Laura. Why don't you
go to the movies?"

I sighed. Dad has loved the woods his whole life.
That's where I get it from. Since I was little, he and I
always roamed the woods for hours and hours,
exploring, talking, laughing. We could always talk
about *anything*.

Now he spent his time locked up in the little shed
in our backyard. And he was always silent or
grouchy.

"I have to work on my science project," I said. I
followed Ellen through the back door.

She's tall and skinny and all legs, like a deer.
With her big, dark eyes and sort of innocent, round
face, Ellen reminds me of a delicate, graceful doe.

If she's a doe, I'm a fox. My red-brown hair is
kind of like fox fur. I'm short and quick, and I have

wide-apart brown eyes and a foxy smile.

I'm always comparing all the kids I know to animals. I guess it's because I love animals so much.

Ellen and I stepped out into a cool, crisp spring day. A string of puffy clouds floated low over the trees. The air smelled fresh and sweet.

"Sorry about Dad," I said to Ellen. "He's so different ever since he left his job at the animal hospital. I'm kind of worried about him."

"Maybe you should call your mother. Ask her for some advice," Ellen suggested.

"I did call her. But she said I needed to be patient. She said leaving a job is a big deal, and he probably needs time to adjust."

"That makes sense," Ellen said.

I frowned. "I wish my mom was here. I really miss her. Phone calls and e-mail just aren't the same."

My mom moved to Chicago after she and Dad divorced five years ago. They gave me a choice—and I chose to live with Dad.

"Some kids might think I made a weird choice," I admitted. "But I could never live in a city. If I didn't live near the woods, I'd go crazy."

"Chicago sounds pretty exciting to me. I'd move there in a minute," Ellen said. She peered into the distance, at a large black bird flapping over the trees.

I watched it, too. Its wings beat rapidly against its body. Hard, almost frantic.

Another bird rose from the treetops. Flying toward

us. Then changing direction abruptly. Flying away. Then back toward us. Frantic. Confused.

The woods echoed with a sharp cry as another bird soared from the treetops. Then a cloud of birds rose up. A dark cloud of beating wings. Beating so hard, it sounded like thunder.

I blinked, startled. "What is going on?" I cried.

More birds flew from the woods. Hundreds of them. Flying in a tight circle. Blocking out the sun. Plunging us into darkness.

Ellen grabbed my arm. "Wow. What *is* that?" she whispered.

"I don't know," I gasped, watching the birds, a black tornado swirling, spinning above the trees. "I've never seen birds swarm like that!"

The birds screeched and cawed. Flying low then rising high, flying round and round, circling the woods, squawking louder with each turn.

I heard the snap of a twig behind me.

I turned and saw that Dad had followed us outside. Behind his thick glasses, he gazed up at the sky. His hand trembled as he pushed a lock of hair from his eyes.

"Something has them stirred up," he whispered. "Something is wrong out there, Laura. Don't go. Don't go into the woods today."

"I—I have to go," I replied. "My project . . ."

Dad stared at the swirling black funnel cloud of shrieking birds. "Birds don't act like that unless something is terribly wrong," he said softly.

And then he took off, running full speed across the back lawn.

"Dad!" I shouted. "Dad—where are you going? Come back!"

He didn't turn around. I watched him vanish into the trees.

"What is he doing?" Ellen asked, her hands pressed to her face.

"I don't know," I said, huddling next to her. We watched the dark cloud of birds, circling, circling. Their shrill, frantic cries echoed in my head.

I raised my hands to my ears to block out the noise—and the cries suddenly stopped. The birds circled now in eerie silence. Their flapping wings slowed.

They swooped down, down to the woods. Hidden by the leafy treetops, they disappeared. The sky glowed in the sunlight again. And once again I could hear the gentle rustle of the wind.

Ellen collapsed onto the grass. "That was so totally scary. Those birds—they seemed really angry. I thought they were going to attack us. But then they just vanished."

"I've never seen anything like that before," I said, my heart pounding. "I'll bet Dad is right. Something stirred them up. But what?"

I cupped my hands around my mouth. "Dad? Where are you?"

No reply.

Ellen climbed to her feet. "Do you still want to take photos?" She brushed her hair back. "Do you think it's safe?"

I stared at the sky over the trees. The sun sparkled brightly. No birds in sight. "We'll be okay," I told her.

Georgie, my German shepherd, came trotting around the side of the house. His tail started wagging when he saw us.

He came running up to me first. He knows I'm his best friend. I grabbed his neck, and we started wrestling on the grass.

"We're bringing Georgie with us—right?" Ellen asked.

I nodded. "Of course. I wouldn't go into the woods

without him. Georgie and I have been exploring the woods together since he was a little puppy."

Ellen led the way across the grass, and I followed after her. The camera bounced against my chest as I walked. "My project is due in less than two weeks," I groaned. "And I hardly have any photos."

My science project was to study the plant and animal life at Luker Pond. I had already photographed the different kinds of plant life. Now I needed to photograph some animal life.

I thought it would be easy. But I had visited the pond every afternoon for a week, and I was having trouble finding animals.

Ellen jogged up to the woods. Her hair swung behind her like a horse's tail. Georgie and I caught up with her at the forest's edge.

She lifted her eyes to the sky above the trees. "What do you think happened?" she asked. "Do you think some big animal frightened the birds from their nests?"

"I don't know," I replied. "And why did my dad—"

I stopped short when I heard the howl.

A high, shrill cry. The sound of an animal in pain.

Georgie raised his head, tensed his back, and started to bark furiously.

The animal howled again.

I stepped into the woods and listened carefully, trying to locate the sound.

Another howl. A wail of agony.

But it wasn't coming from the woods.

I spun around. "Whoa. It's coming from the garden shed," I said, pointing.

The shed is square and wood-shingled. It stands halfway between the house and the woods. It's nearly as big as a one-car garage, with a solid wood door and a flat roof.

"What's in there?" Ellen asked. "What is crying like that?"

"I don't know," I told her. "Dad won't let me go near it."

Ellen squinted hard at the shed. The howling finally stopped. "Laura, I don't want you to take this the wrong way—but it's getting kind of creepy around your house."

I laughed.

"What kind of work is he doing in there?" She continued to stare at the shed.

I sighed. "Some kind of research, I guess. He gets too weird when I ask him about it, so I'm not exactly sure. I tried to go in and take a look last week. But he keeps the door locked."

I leaned down and petted Georgie. Then we stepped into the shade of the forest, onto a winding dirt path that curved through the tall trees.

"Why did your dad leave his job at the animal hospital?" Ellen asked. "Was he fired?"

"I don't know," I said, pushing a low branch out of the way. "He won't tell me. He hardly speaks to me anymore. I don't know what to think."

Ellen's eyes flashed. She grabbed my arm. "I know what happened, Laura." A sly grin spread over her face. "I know why he left his job. Your dad and Dr. Carpenter were going out—and she dumped him!"

"YUCK!" I exclaimed. I put my finger down my throat and pretended to puke. "That is *so* not what happened," I said. "Dad and Dr. Carpenter? No way."

Dad and Dr. Carpenter have known each other for four years, ever since she moved here to run the animal hospital. If she and Dad had some kind of romance going on, I'd know about it.

"You're wrong," I said. "They never went out on a single date or anything."

"But she comes to your house all the time," Ellen argued.

"Not anymore," I murmured.

Dr. Carpenter used to come over a few times a week. We'd all hang out together. Watch videos or play Scrabble. Dad liked to make up crazy words to try to trick Dr. C. It was a lot of fun.

I loved her visits. It was great to have someone I could talk to about stuff—friends, clothes, teachers.

"I'm telling you—she dumped him!" Ellen insisted.

Dad and Dr. Carpenter? I didn't think so.

But then why *did* Dad leave the animal hospital? Dr. Carpenter said Dad was the best vet in the world.

She wouldn't fire him—would she?

We climbed over a fallen tree, blanketed with thick green and yellow fungus. We were almost to the pond.

"Let's talk about this fabulous birthday party I'm throwing for you," I said. I wanted to change the subject. "I need a list. Who do you want me to invite?"

"Only boys," Ellen replied. She grinned.

"You're joking, right?" I said.

"Why don't you invite that guy you met, Joe?" Ellen suggested. "I'd really like to meet him."

"Hey!" I said sharply. "I saw him first!"

I turned and saw Georgie examining a pile of dead leaves. Sniffing hard, he started to paw furiously at the leaf pile.

"Georgie—get away from there!" I shouted. "Georgie—no!"

Ellen made a disgusted face. "Whoa. What is he doing?"

Ellen doesn't really like being outdoors that much. She doesn't like dirt, bugs, or forest animals. She'd much rather be home, reading a book or writing in her diary. She's a great writer, and she's the editor of our school newspaper.

But because she's such a good friend, she goes into the woods with me to keep me company.

"Georgie—get away from there!" I shouted.

The dog ignored me. Grunting, he buried his head in the fat pile of brown leaves—and pulled out something in his teeth.

"What *is* that?" Ellen cried. She pressed her hands to the sides of her face. "What has he got?"

"Let me see it, Georgie," I said, stepping toward him, reaching out my hand. "Drop. Drop it, boy. What have you got?"

I edged closer. "What is it, boy? What do you have there?"

The dog let out a grunt. Then his jaw snapped open, and the object dropped to the ground.

Ellen and I stared down at it—and we both began to scream.

"It's—it's a finger!" I cried. "A human finger!"

Georgie barked at it, his tail wagging furiously. Then he took off, heading home.

"Oh, gross," Ellen moaned, shutting her eyes. "Is it really a finger? I'm going to be totally sick."

I stepped up to it and poked it with my shoe. I squatted down to see it better.

"Yes, it's a finger," I said weakly. My stomach lurched. I studied it. "But . . . maybe it's not from a person."

Ellen had her hands over her face, and she had turned away. "Wh-what do you mean?"

"Well . . . the skin is kind of leathery. And the fingernail is pointed. And it's so hairy. . . ."

"SHUT UP!" Ellen screamed. "Don't talk about it anymore! Let's just get away from it." She started back to the path. But I didn't get up. I stared at the finger more closely.

"Strange," I murmured. "It's really ragged at the end. It looks like it was torn off."

"Just shut up about it," Ellen said. "I feel sick. Really."

"Here. Catch!" I shouted. I pretended to toss it to her.

She screamed and ducked, even though I didn't have anything in my hand. "Not funny, Laura," she muttered. "Hey—why don't you take a photo of it? For your science project."

"I'm supposed to photograph whole animals," I said. "Not just parts."

But I should take it home, I thought. Show it to Dad. Maybe he knew what kind of animal had fingers like this.

I didn't want to freak Ellen out. So while she wasn't looking, I picked up the finger. I kept it hidden in my palm so she wouldn't see it.

Ellen and I wandered through the woods. White moths fluttered over Luker Pond. High in a tree, I heard the *knock-knock-knock* of a woodpecker. Yes! Excellent! I *needed* that woodpecker! I raised the camera to my eye and searched the tree for it.

"I've got to go," Ellen said. "What time is it, anyway?"

I studied the trees through the camera viewfinder. "Close to three, I think."

"Oh, wow. I've *really* got to go," Ellen said. "I promised Stevie Palmer I'd play tennis with him at three." She jumped over a flat stone and started to jog away.

Stevie Palmer—blond hair, blue eyes, great athlete—Ellen's latest crush.

"And don't forget to invite Stevie to my party!" she shouted.

"No, wait!" I cried, lowering the camera. "Who else should I invite? Who else?"

She turned back, pulling her hair behind her shoulder. "Invite *everybody*!" she yelled. Then she disappeared behind a stand of evergreen shrubs.

I wish she didn't have to go, I thought, circling the pond. I was alone in the woods, and for the first time in my life I felt tense about it.

I'll feel better once I take some photographs, I decided. I had taken only three or four. I desperately needed to find some animals—or my project was going to be completely lame.

I stepped up to the edge of the pond. Come on, animals. Where are you hiding?

I was so desperate, I snapped a picture of the white moths fluttering above the water.

I'll sit down and wait, I decided. Maybe if I'm really still, a deer will come to drink.

I sat down. And waited. I held my camera in my lap and listened to the whisper of the trees. One of my favorite sounds.

A minute later I heard another sound, this time behind me. It was the snap of a twig.

I turned around but didn't see anything.

I stood up. And heard the heavy scrape of hooves.

Was it a deer?

The sounds stopped.

I turned and took a few steps forward.

Behind me, I heard the footsteps again.

I stopped. And once more the footsteps stopped.

I shuddered as a tingle of fear ran down my back.

I'm never frightened in the woods. Never. Even when I'm by myself.

But today was different.

I pictured the circling birds . . . the ugly finger in the grass . . . I heard my dad's warning to stay away. . . .

And now something was trailing me. Something was creeping up behind me.

"Dad?" I called.

No answer.

I listened hard. I heard the excited chitter of birds in a high tree limb. The whisper of wind. The creak of a branch.

Holding my breath, I took another step. Another.

I was listening for the footsteps. And I heard them. The heavy thud of shoes or hooves.

With a gasp, I spun around quickly.

"Wh-who's there?" I cried.

A boy stepped out from the trees. He gazed at me shyly, then lowered his dark eyes. He was short and kind of chubby. He had long, black tangles of hair, very shiny, nearly as long as Ellen's.

"Joe—hi!" I called. I breathed a sigh of relief.

"Hey, it's you!" he said, trotting up to me.

I smiled at him. "I heard something following me. I—I didn't know what to think."

Pink circles appeared on his cheeks. "It's only me," he said softly.

He's so shy, I realized. And really cute.

He wore baggy denim cutoffs and a black T-shirt. A long silver chain dangled around his neck. In his right hand he carried a fishing pole.

He pointed to my camera. "Snap anything today?"

"No, I . . . " I glanced down and suddenly realized I was holding the disgusting finger. If Joe sees it, he'll think I'm totally weird, I decided.

"I heard a woodpecker in that tree over there," I said, pointing.

When Joe turned to the tree, I let the finger fall from my hand. He turned back—and I stamped my shoe down over it.

"I'm desperate," I said. "Where are the animals? Are they all on strike?"

"Maybe we could drag some over," Joe said. "You know. Go to a pet store or something. Get some hamsters or turtles and bring them to the pond."

"I don't think so," I said, laughing. "But keep thinking."

We stepped up to the pond. Joe kicked a stone into the water. His long hair fluttered in the wind.

"Catch anything today?" I asked. The last time I met Joe in the woods, I found him sitting on a flat rock, fishing in a stream. He told me he loved to fish, but he never ate what he caught. He always threw the fish back. That made me like him even more.

"No. No luck today," he said. "I'll try again tomorrow."

"So how are things at Wilberne Academy?" I asked. I admit it. I had a little bit of a sneer on my face.

He turned to me. "You're making fun of me because I go to a private school, aren't you!"

"No way!" I insisted. "It's just . . . well . . . the guys I know from Wilberne are such snobs. And you don't seem like that."

He snickered. "Hey, thanks. I think."

I decided I'd invite Joe to Ellen's birthday party. The idea made my heart start to pound. I realized I was suddenly nervous.

Go ahead, Laura. Just invite him, I told myself. Don't make a big deal about it. Be bold—like Ellen.

I took a deep breath. "Uh . . . Joe?"

Two chattering birds interrupted. They were so loud, right above our heads. I turned in time to see them take off, chirping together as they flew.

They were joined by three or four other chattering birds. What a racket! They formed a ragged V and flew out of sight.

Joe shook his head. "What's *their* problem?"

We laughed together. I liked the way Joe's eyes narrowed into little moon slivers when he laughed. He reminded me of a bear—a little, friendly bear you see in cartoons.

I decided to try again. "Uh . . . I'm giving a party for my friend . . . " I started.

I didn't have a chance to finish.

Everything seemed to explode at once. Trees shook. Animals cried out. Birds cawed and squawked.

The sky blackened as birds took off, flapping their wings wildly. The grass bent as field mice stampeded past our feet.

"Wh-what's happening?" I cried.

Joe spun around, his eyes wide with fright and confusion.

The sky grew even blacker, as if night had fallen.

A shrill, chittering squeal rang out, echoing off the trees. And over the whistlelike cries came the furious flapping of wings.

"Bats!" Joe cried.

Yes. Bats—hundreds of bats—swarmed above us, squealing, swooping high, then darting into the trees.

"But—but—" I sputtered. "Bats don't fly in the daylight!"

I gasped as a bat swooped over my head. I felt its dry, sharp wing scrape against my face, felt a blast of hot wind off its body.

"Get down, Laura!" Joe grabbed me by the shoulders and pushed me to the ground.

"Get down! Cover your head! They're ATTACKING!"

"Cover your head! Cover your head!"

Those were the last words I heard. The flapping wings drowned out Joe's screams. The shrill bat cries seemed to pierce my eardrums.

I pressed myself into a tight ball and covered my head with both hands. "Ohhh." I let out a terrified moan as bat wings slapped my back and shoulders.

This can't be happening! I thought, shuddering. Bats don't come out during the day.

What is going on?

I felt the beating of wings against my hands. Felt a sharp tug on my scalp.

"Leave me alone!" I screamed, frantically brushing two bats from my hair.

All around me—all *over* me—the beating wings, the scrape of talons, and the cries . . . the shrill siren cries.

No—please—no, I silently prayed. Go away. Go away!

I tried to stay curled in a tight ball. But each slap of a bat wing, each thud of a bat slamming into me, each scratch of a bat talon against my clothing made me squirm in horror.

"Joe—are you okay?" I shouted. "Joe—?"

No answer.

And then the shrill squeals began to fade. The sound of beating wings rose up, away from me.

"Joe?" I cried, still afraid to open my eyes. "Joe? Why don't you answer me?"

"Joe?"

Bat wings flapped in the distance now. The shrill cries faded and died.

Trembling, still hunched into a tight ball, I slowly opened my eyes. And raised my head.

And screamed again.

Beside me, Joe was hunched on his knees, battling two large bats.

One bat had its talons stuck in Joe's thick hair. It batted its wings furiously, shrieking, struggling to pull free.

The other bat clung to the neck of Joe's T-shirt. Its outspread wings blocked Joe's face from view.

But I could hear his desperate cries.

He swiped at the bats with both hands.

The bats shrieked and flapped.

Joe toppled onto his back. He wrapped a hand around the bat at his throat. Squeezed until the bat grew silent.

The curled talons loosened. Joe heaved the bat into the trees.

The other bat clung to his hair.

I stood frozen in horror, watching Joe struggle. Then I finally managed to move. I dived to the ground—and reached for the flapping bat.

"NO!" Joe screamed. "GET AWAY!" Then he rolled over in the dirt. Grabbed the bat with both hands. And carefully pried it from his hair.

The bat squawked and squealed.

Joe heaved it aside. Before I could say anything, he leaped to his feet and started to run.

"Joe—" I called. "Stop!"

He stopped on the far side of a small clearing. His face was bright red. He was gasping for breath.

"Don't go. My house is right over there," I said. "My dad is a doctor. I mean, he's a vet. But he knows about bats. Let him take a look at your cuts and scratches."

"No," Joe said, shaking his head. His hands clutched the sides of his hair. "I—I mean, no thanks."

"Is your head cut? Did they scratch you?" I asked.

"I think I'm okay," he insisted. "Anyway, my mother is home. She'll take me to the doctor."

"No—wait," I said. "If you're cut, you should see someone right now. Come with me. My dad will—"

"No. I'm okay. Really." He turned away. And still

holding his head, he started to run. Just before he disappeared into the thickening woods, he called, "See you soon."

"Wait!" I shouted. I forced the words out. "I want to invite you to a party! Joe!"

But he was gone.

I sighed. I stood there staring after him. I could hear the flap of bat wings in the distance.

My whole body itched. I could still feel their talons scratching my clothes, could still feel the air off their fluttering wings.

Something got them riled up, I thought. Like the birds earlier this afternoon.

Something in these woods frightened them. Something made them act totally weird.

But what?

A few minutes later I stepped out of the woods, into our backyard. The shed door was shut tight. Dad had returned. I could hear him banging around inside.

I was desperate to tell him about the bat attack. If I had been scratched or bitten I would have, but I wasn't. Plus, I knew when he was in the shed, he didn't want to be disturbed. So I went inside to start dinner.

Usually Dad and I took turns making dinner, or we'd make up new recipes together, and it was fun. Sometimes Dr. Carpenter would join in. I really missed her. I realized now that Dr. C. had sort of become my fill-in mom.

I pulled a chicken from the refrigerator, dug my hand into the chicken, and started to pull out the gunky stuff inside.

Through the kitchen window, I could see the woods. Quiet now. The trees swaying softly, darkening as the sun went down.

The phone rang. I jerked my hand out of the chicken and tried to wipe the guts off on a dish towel.

Then I picked up the phone. "Hello?"

It was Ellen. "Laura—where have you been? I've been calling you for half an hour."

"In the woods," I said. "It was so weird, Ellen. I—"

"Don't invite Stevie to my birthday party," she interrupted.

"Excuse me?"

"Erase him from the list," she said. "What a creep. Just because I'm half an hour late for our tennis match, he throws a fit. Then he tried to slam the ball down my throat all afternoon."

"Ellen—" I started.

"Can I help it if I beat him in three straight sets? He is *so* not mature, Laura. And when I offered to give him tennis lessons, he called me a bunch of babyish names and stomped away."

I laughed.

"Just cross him off the list. Okay?" Ellen snapped.

"No problem," I said. "Hey—you just missed Joe. He was in the woods."

"Oh, wow," she muttered. "I really wanted to

meet him. Did you invite him to the party?"

"I—I tried," I said. "But—"

"Oh, I've got to go," Ellen interrupted. "My brothers are fighting upstairs, and I'm in charge."

She clicked off before I could say another word.

I set the phone down and stuck my hand back in the chicken.

A short while later dinner was ready. I'd made a green salad, baked potatoes, and string beans to go with the chicken.

I carried everything to the table, then glanced at the clock. Nearly seven, and still no Dad.

What was he doing? Did he completely lose track of the time?

I stared out the kitchen window at the shed. I didn't want dinner to get cold. And I was so eager to tell Dad about the strange bat attack and the creepy finger I found.

I pulled open the back door, cupped my hands around my mouth, and called to him.

No reply.

Two robins lifted their heads and stared at me. I started to jog across the grass, and they flew away.

"Hey—Dad?" I called, stepping up to the shed door. A sharp, chemical smell floated out from the shed. Like the smell in a doctor's office. I heard a soft, whimpering noise coming from inside.

I tried the door. To my surprise, it wasn't locked.

"Dad?" I pushed the door open just a crack.

I glimpsed a lot of equipment, stacked to the ceiling. What was Dad holding between his hands? What was making those noises?

A small pink animal.

He gripped the animal in one hand—and was about to give it an injection with an enormous hypodermic needle.

"Dad? What are you doing?" I called.

He spun around, and his expression turned to rage. "Get out!" he screamed. "Out! Get out of here! Don't ever open that door!"

I backed away with a gasp and pulled the door shut. I'd never seen him become so furious.

My legs trembled as I stepped away from the door.

Why did he yell at me like that?

Why was he acting this way?

My eyes filled with tears.

In the past few weeks my father had become a complete stranger to me.

I felt so alone. So totally alone—and frightened of my own father.

Dad and I ate in silence for a while. He kept his eyes on his plate and shoveled down his food quickly, as if trying to get dinner over with.

The only sounds were the clink of our silverware and the raspy *caw caw caw* of the injured crow in my bedroom.

"I'm sorry." Dad finally raised his eyes to me. "I didn't mean to shout at you."

I took a deep breath. "Why *did* you scream like that?" I asked.

He scratched his graying hair, studying me. "I'm doing very important work," he said. "And I can't have any interruptions. The timing is so important."

Dad stood up to clear the table. "I know I've been very tense lately. I know I haven't been paying much attention to you. But things are going to get better. I promise." Dad smiled for the first time in weeks. "How about a game of Scrabble?"

Dad and I moved into the living room and set up

the Scrabble board. He started making up crazy words, and I did, too. And suddenly everything seemed back to normal again.

So I thought it would be okay to ask him a question. "Dad, exactly what kind of work are you doing?"

He swallowed. His cheek twitched. "I can't talk about it."

"Why not? Don't you trust me, Dad?"

"I can't talk about it. Until it is completed, I can't discuss it with anyone." He sighed.

"But—" I started to protest.

He pulled off his glasses and placed them down on the table. "No more questions, okay? There's nothing more to say," he said softly.

"I'm not a baby," I said, my voice trembling. "If you're doing some kind of secret work, you can trust me."

"I'm sorry, Laura. I really can't discuss it with you."

Dad leaned back in his chair. He closed his eyes as if he was suddenly exhausted. Then he opened them. "Want to finish this game?" he asked.

I nodded, even though it was the last thing I wanted to do.

When we finished playing, Dad helped me put the game away. "Laura, it might be a good idea if you lived with your mother for a while," he said. He kept his eyes down on the Scrabble box.

I grabbed my chest as if I'd been stabbed.

Those words hurt so much.

"You—you want to send me away?" I choked out.

"It might be best."

"I have to move away because . . . because I asked you what you're doing in the shed?" I said, trying to force back the tears.

"You'll understand someday," he said quietly. He pulled his glasses back on. "It's for your own good."

"No!" I screamed. "No! How can it be for my own good? You know I don't want to live in Chicago. I have to be near the woods. And what about my school? And all my friends? I can't just leave them because you have some kind of stupid secret!"

"Laura—" Dad raised a hand to silence me. "I'm your father. I have to do what's best for you. Believe me, I don't want to send you away. I love you more than anything, but . . . "

I pressed my hand over my mouth to hold back a sob.

I can't believe he is saying this, I thought, unable to stop my whole body from trembling.

"Okay, okay," I finally choked out. "I won't go near the shed. I promise. And I won't ask any more questions. No more questions about your work."

Dad squinted at me. "You promise?"

"Promise," I said.

But there was no way I was keeping that promise!

I'm going to learn his secret, I decided. I'm going to find out what's the big deal. What's so secret that he'd send his own daughter away?

I'm going to find out the truth.

I went to bed a little after eleven. But I couldn't fall asleep.

I was too hurt to sleep. Too hurt and frightened and angry—all at the same time.

I reached for the phone on my night table and called Ellen. "Hello." Her voice was groggy with sleep.

"Did I wake you?" I asked.

"It's okay." She yawned. "What's wrong? You sound terrible."

I told her about what Dad had said to me. "I can't sleep," I whispered. "Every time I shut my eyes, a new horror scene appears in my mind. I keep picturing my dad in his white lab coat. Holding a helpless little animal in one hand and a huge hypodermic needle in the other. Injecting little animals with strange chemicals. Making them whimper and howl."

"But your dad is a vet," Ellen said. "He gives shots to animals all the time."

I stared up at the shadows on my bedroom ceiling, my mind spinning. "But it's different now," I said. "He won't tell me what he's doing. What kind of experiments would have to be a secret—from his own daughter?"

"I don't know. But your dad wouldn't hurt a fly. He could never torture an animal. It's impossible."

"Ellen, he lost his job at the animal hospital. Maybe it was because he was doing something wrong," I said.

"You don't know that," she argued. I knew she was trying to calm me down. But nothing she said made me feel better.

I finally let her go back to sleep. Then I closed my eyes and fell asleep, too—but not for long.

A low rumbling sound floated in through my open bedroom window and woke me up.

I glanced at my clock radio. A little before two in the morning.

Rubbing my eyes, I crept to the window and gazed out at the woods. Darting lights flickered through the trees.

I forced back a yawn and stared hard. The lights swept slowly back and forth, floating eerily like ghosts. A shiver ran down my back.

There are no roads in the woods. And no other houses for nearly a mile. Who could be out there?

I'd better wake up Dad, I thought. I turned away from the window.

34

No. I changed my mind. I'm not going to wake him up. I don't really want to talk to him now.

But I had to find out who was out in the woods. I pulled on the jeans and tank top I'd worn during the day. A few seconds later I opened the kitchen door and stepped outside.

Clouds drifted across the sliver of a moon. A shifting wind made the grass bend first one way, then the other. Like ocean waves, I thought. It was a warm breeze, but it sent a chill down my back.

I carefully shut the door, listening for its soft click, making sure it was closed. Then I trotted across the lawn toward the woods.

I searched the trees for the lights. But they had vanished. The rumbling sound had also stopped.

"Weird," I muttered.

I stopped halfway across the yard and listened. Silence now. Silence . . .

Except for a low cry.

A sad whimper.

I turned. The cries were coming from the shed.

The shed. I had to see what was inside it. This was the perfect time.

Dad kept a padlock on the door. But I knew where he hid the key. I crept back into the kitchen and pulled the key from the little cup where Mom used to keep her Sweet'n Low packets.

Then I sneaked back outside. I felt a chill of fear as I stepped up to the shed. I could hear the animals inside, groaning, crying. It sounded as if they were pleading with me to rescue them.

"I'm coming," I whispered.

But I wheeled away from the door when I heard another sound.

A low growl. And then the pounding *thud* of heavy footsteps.

Running. Running rapidly toward me.

I was too startled to move. I froze as the big creature appeared from around the side of the shed.

It took a powerful leap. Leaped high. Caught me at the shoulders.

And knocked me hard to the ground.

"Georgie!" I cried. "Get off! Get off me!"

Tail wagging furiously, the big dog pinned me to the ground and licked my face. His hot breath steamed my cheeks. I was laughing too hard to roll away from him.

"Georgie—stop!" I pleaded. "Are you lonely out here? Is that the problem?"

Finally I pushed him away. I sat up and wiped the thick slobber off my cheeks.

A light washed over me. I turned to the window and saw the kitchen lights on. The back door swung open. Dad poked his head out. He held his pajama bottoms up with one hand and squinted into the yard. He didn't have his glasses on.

"Laura?" Dad called, his voice clogged with sleep. "What are you doing out here in the middle of the night?"

"There were lights," I said. "In the woods. And I heard some kind of rumbling sound. I—I wanted to see what it was."

Dad scratched his forehead. His graying hair was sticking out all over his head. "You were probably dreaming," he said, frowning.

"No. It was real," I insisted. "The lights were moving around the trees, and—"

"Come inside," he said. He squinted at me. "You weren't trying to sneak into the shed, were you?"

"No. Of course not," I lied. I had the padlock key wrapped tightly in my fist.

For a moment his stare turned cold. I felt as if his eyes were stabbing me. "Come inside," he repeated. "I don't want to hear about lights in the trees. I'm tired."

I sighed and slumped into the house. I could see there was no point in trying to talk to him.

Once Dad went upstairs I slipped the key back into its normal place. I glanced out the kitchen window and stared at the shed. I could still hear the mournful cries. Suddenly I knew where I could find some answers.

The animal hospital.

I'll go see Dr. Carpenter at the animal hospital tomorrow, I decided. I know she and Dad aren't talking, but that doesn't mean I can't talk to her.

She'll tell me the truth about Dad. I know she will.

•   •   •

After school the next day I loaded up my backpack, pushed my way through a crowd of kids, and ran out the front door of the school building.

It was about a two-mile walk to the animal hospital, and I wanted to get there before Dr. Carpenter left for the day.

The animal hospital was tucked in a cul-de-sac at the other side of the woods. It was an enormous two-story white stucco building with a steeply sloping red roof.

It had started as a small, square building and had quickly grown. Now it had endless wings, annexes, and research labs, stretching in all directions into the woods.

Inside, it looked more like an old hotel than a hospital. The long halls twisted and turned and seemed to stretch for miles. The doors were made of black oak and creaked when you opened them. The walls were painted dark green. A crystal chandelier hung over the waiting room, which was furnished with old brown leather armchairs and sofas.

Since it didn't look like an animal hospital, it was always surprising to hear the barks and yowls and chirps of the patients.

I had seen the operating rooms a few times when I visited Dad. They were white and bright and sparkling clean. And the research labs were also very modern and medical looking.

As I stepped into the waiting room, a flood of memories swept over me. I remembered so many visits here. And several really upsetting scenes. . . .

I remembered an adorable white-and-brown cocker spaniel puppy that had been hit by a car. And a bright red-and-blue macaw that had an ear of corn stuck in its throat. And two huge yellow dogs who started a snarling, raging fight in the waiting room, clawing each other until the carpet was puddled with blood.

The waiting room was empty now. I glanced at the clock above the reception desk: a little after four-thirty. A young woman sat behind the desk, shuffling through folders.

I asked to see Dr. Carpenter and told her my name. She picked up the phone, pushed a few buttons, and muttered into the receiver.

A few seconds later Dr. Carpenter came sweeping into the room, her white lab coat flying behind her. "Laura! How nice to see you!" she cried and wrapped me in a hug. "How are you? I've missed you so much!"

I hugged her back, taking in her pretty blond hair, her bright green eyes that always seemed to catch the light, and her warm smile. I missed her, too.

I remembered sometimes when I was angry at Mom, I secretly wished that Dr. Carpenter was my mother instead.

I glanced behind her, where a quarter, a dime,

and a penny, mounted on black velvet and set in a small silver picture frame, hung on the wall. It made me smile. It reminded me of Dr. C.'s first day at the animal hospital, four years ago.

Georgie had swallowed some change I had dropped on the kitchen floor, and he got really sick. Dr. Carpenter operated, and it was a great success! She framed the change—because it was from her very first patient.

Dr. Carpenter laughed and twirled me around, as if I were still a little girl. "Laura, did you stop by just to say hi?"

I hesitated. "Well . . . no." My smile faded. "I really wanted to talk to you. I mean, if you have time."

I suddenly felt nervous. Could I really ask her to tell me the truth about Dad?

"I seem to have plenty of time," she replied. She gestured around the empty waiting room. "I've been spending more and more time in the research lab. Kind of frustrating. But it's important."

She put a hand on my shoulder and guided me through the door, down a long hall with closed doors on both sides. Her office stood at the end of the hall. She gestured for me to take a seat in a low blue armchair in front of her desk.

The desk was glass, clean and uncluttered except for one stack of papers and folders, and a telephone. The walls were covered with framed photos of animals, some of the pets she had cared for.

Dr. Carpenter slid gracefully into the desk chair and swept her blond hair back over her shoulders. Then she leaned across the glass desk and smiled at me.

"This is such a surprise," she said. "I'm so happy that you came to see me. What did you want to talk about, Laura? Is it boy trouble? Something you can't discuss with your father?"

I laughed. I'm not sure why. The laugh just burst out.

"Do you get to talk to your mother much?" Dr. Carpenter asked. Elbows on the desk, she rested her head in her hands, studying me with those intense green eyes. "How is she doing?"

I shrugged. "She calls once a week. And I visit her a lot," I said. "But she's so far away. It's not like having a mom who's always there for you. . . ." My voice trailed off.

Dr. Carpenter frowned. "I know what you mean. Well, how is Ellen? Who is she in love with this week?" Dr. Carpenter laughed.

"Last week it was Steve, the tennis player. This week—I'm not sure." I laughed, too.

"So what are you and your dad up to these days? You two still making up Scrabble words? Still taking long walks in the woods?"

I took a deep breath. "We don't really play Scrabble all that much. We hardly do anything together lately."

My throat suddenly felt so dry. I coughed. "He's—I don't know—different lately."

Dr. Carpenter's eyebrows went up. "Different? What do you mean? How is he different?"

"Well . . . he's very quiet and . . . angry. He hardly talks to me. He—he spends a lot of time alone, working in the shed."

"Hmmm. That doesn't sound like your dad at all. What is he working on?" Dr. Carpenter asked.

"I don't know. He won't tell me," I replied.

Dr. Carpenter reached across the desk and squeezed my hand. "Laura, he's probably just out of sorts. Leaving a job isn't easy. You have to give him time."

I swallowed hard. "I . . . wanted to ask you about that. Why . . . why *did* my dad leave?"

Dr. Carpenter released my hand. She leaned back in her chair and sighed.

"Please tell me," I pleaded. "Why did my dad leave the animal hospital?"

"I had to let him go," Dr. Carpenter said finally.

I gasped. "You mean—you fired him?"

She sat up straight. Her cheeks reddened. "Well . . . that's not really the right word. I had to let him go because—"

"Why?" I interrupted. "Why?"

She swallowed. "It's hard to explain, Laura. We . . . had different goals. We wanted to take our research in different directions."

I let out a deep breath. Different goals, I thought. That seemed okay.

Suddenly I felt all the tension leave my body. It was good to have someone to talk to. I knew coming here was the right thing to do.

I sat back in my chair. "What kind of work is Dad—" I started to ask another question, but the phone rang.

"Sorry," she said, making a face at the phone. She picked up the receiver and talked for two or three minutes. "No, you shouldn't bathe him," she kept saying. "Keep the fur dry. I know, I know. You'll have to put up with the smell. No. You shouldn't bathe him."

After a few more minutes she hung up the phone and stood up. "I'm sorry, Laura. I'd better get back to work. But come back anytime. Really. I mean it. I've missed you."

We said our goodbyes and I left.

Outside, heavy clouds had rolled over the sun, and the air had turned cold. Wisps of fog floated low to the ground.

Visiting Dr. Carpenter was a good idea. But I still felt so confused. I wasn't any closer to finding out why Dad was acting so strange.

When I reached home, I headed to the shed. I put my ear to the door. Quiet. Dad wasn't in there. I yanked hard on the lock.

"You won't get it open that way."

I jumped back in surprise as Joe jogged out from the woods.

He grinned at me. "I think a key would work better."

I laughed. I was glad to see him. He looked really cute in baggy denim shorts and a faded red T-shirt.

This time I'm definitely going to invite him to the birthday party, I decided. "What are you doing here?" I asked.

He shrugged. "I was exploring, you know. I spotted

the back of the house from the woods, but I didn't know it was yours."

He grinned and swept back his long hair with both hands. "You should have come to the pond today. I saw a whole family of deer there."

I rolled my eyes. "Of course. The deer come when I'm not there. They don't want me to get an A."

We both turned when we heard a growl coming from the trees.

A dog's growl.

Georgie loped to the edge of the clearing. He stopped a few feet from us and raised his head, big, brown eyes studying us suspiciously.

"Hey—where'd you come from, boy?" Joe asked.

"Georgie!" I called. "What were you doing in the woods?"

Georgie's tail began to wag. He lowered his head again and trotted up to us. Dead leaves clung to the fur on his side.

I reached to pull them off. Then I tried to hug him, but he pulled away. "Georgie, what's wrong?" I asked. "Aren't you glad to see me?"

Georgie bumped up to Joe and sniffed his khaki shorts, making loud snuffling sounds.

Joe laughed and jumped back. "Hey, stop! That tickles! You have a crazy dog, Laura!"

I bent down. "Georgie, what's wrong? Come over to me."

He pressed his wet snout against my arm and

sniffed hard. Then he began to sniff the legs of my jeans.

To my surprise, he let out an angry growl.

His back stiffened. He backed up, glaring angrily at Joe and me. Then he pulled back his lips and bared his teeth.

"Georgie—are you crazy? What's wrong, boy?" I cried. I turned to Joe. "He's the most gentle dog in the world. Really."

Joe took a step back. "Someone forgot to tell him that!"

"Easy, boy," I said to Georgie, still crouched down. "Easy now. What's wrong, boy?" I asked softly, soothingly.

The dog gnashed his teeth and began to snarl. Frightening, harsh growls from deep in his throat.

He lowered his head, eyes wild now, glaring up at us.

"Easy, boy . . . " I whispered. My legs suddenly felt rubbery and weak. "Georgie . . . it's me. . . . It's me. . . ."

Baring his teeth, Georgie opened his mouth in a terrifying growl. His fur bristled. His whole body tensed—and he leaped to attack.

I didn't back away. I didn't move. I tried not to show how afraid I was.

Georgie stopped inches from me, snapping his jaws.

"Easy . . . easy," I whispered. "Good dog. You're a good dog."

Looking up, I glimpsed Joe, his face tight with fear. He had backed away to the edge of the clearing.

"Laura . . . " he called. "Get up. Get away from him."

The dog snarled furiously. His sides heaved in and out as he breathed, wheezing noisily. White drool ran down the front of his open snout.

"Good dog . . . good boy . . . Georgie, it's me. . . . It's me. . . ."

I couldn't crouch there any longer. My legs were trembling too hard. I couldn't hold myself up.

With a cry, I toppled backward. I landed hard. Sitting on the grass. I was practically eye to eye with the snarling creature.

His jagged teeth were inches from my face. Fat globs of drool ran down his open mouth and splattered on the grass.

"Please—" I cried. I raised both hands as if to shield myself from the attack.

Joe came rushing forward. "Get away! GET! GET!" he shouted. He swung both arms wildly and screamed at the top of his lungs.

To my surprise, Georgie stopped snarling. He gazed up at Joe and uttered a pained whimper. He appeared to deflate. All of his muscles went soft.

As I stared in surprise, the dog lowered his head and turned away from us. His tail was tucked tightly between his legs, and his ears went flat against his head.

Whimpering, he slunk away.

"Georgie? Georgie?" I choked out. I sat on the ground, frozen. My mouth was so dry, I couldn't swallow. My whole body shuddered.

"He's never acted that way before," I said, hugging myself tightly, trying to stop myself from shaking.

Joe helped me to my feet. "That was really your dog? What was his problem?" he cried.

"I—I don't know," I said. "Maybe he—he smelled something," I choked out.

"Smelled something on *us*?" Joe asked. "Like what?"

I shook my head. My heart stopped thudding

against my chest. I started to feel a little more normal. "Beats me," I said. "Maybe he smelled something on my jeans."

Joe squinted at me. "Your jeans?"

"Maybe he smelled something from the animal hospital on them. I was just there. The hospital always makes Georgie nervous—ever since his operation."

I told Joe about the time Georgie swallowed the thirty-six cents.

Joe continued to study me. He didn't say anything for a long moment. He appeared to be thinking hard. "What were you doing at the animal hospital?"

I pulled a spider off the sleeve of my T-shirt. "You have to promise not to tell my dad," I said.

Joe laughed. "I don't know your dad."

"Well, you have to promise not to tell anyway," I insisted. "I just went to see someone there. Someone I could talk to. About things."

Joe nodded. He shifted his weight from one foot to the other. "Hope your dog is okay," he said finally. "I'm—I'm glad I know where you live." He started walking toward the woods. Then he broke into a run.

The party, I thought. With all the fright over Georgie, I forgot about inviting him. "Hey, Joe—" I raced after him.

"Got to hurry!" he shouted back. "My parents hate when I'm late for dinner. Catch you later!" He vanished into the trees.

I didn't even get his phone number, I thought. How stupid is that?

I heard the crunch of leaves. Yes! He's coming back, I thought. I'll ask him to the party *and* get his phone number.

I stared and waited, but Joe didn't appear.

I listened. Silence now—and then a voice. A man's voice.

I walked deeper into the woods, following the sound.

Something dropped to the ground with a crash—and I gasped. I moved in closer—and saw it.

The front of a Jeep. It was painted green and brown, camouflage colors. It blended in with the trees perfectly.

An army truck, I thought.

I took a few steps closer. Now I could see the entire vehicle. It wasn't an army truck. It was a large, covered Jeep with a trailer behind it, also painted in camouflage.

The Jeep had huge tires and heavy bumpers. It was parked in the path that curved toward Luker Pond.

The trailer was nearly as big as a moving van, with the top poking up into the trees.

I stepped cautiously closer. The driver's door on the Jeep was hidden by a tree trunk, so I couldn't see if anyone was inside.

As I drew closer, I heard a heavy *thump thump*.

Startled, I flattened my back against a tree.

Thump thummmmp.

Something in the trailer was beating against the trailer's side. Or kicking it. An animal.

I gasped when I heard the cry. A pained cry.

Thump thump thummmp.

It kicked again, uttering another low cry.

I stopped and stared, listening to the creature struggle.

Why was this vehicle out here in the middle of the woods?

And why was there an animal howling inside it?

I circled around the back of the trailer—and saw two men. Both wore blue denim overalls and pale blue workshirts. They were sitting on a large rock, chatting and chewing away on long submarine sandwiches.

One of them swatted a horsefly on top of his head. His head was shaved, completely bald. The other man was very fat and had a blue baseball cap pulled down over long, straggly coppery hair.

I started to walk up to them. I wanted to ask what they had in the truck.

But then I saw their rifles, propped against a tree trunk behind them.

I pulled back. A chill ran down my spine. It wasn't hunting season. Why did they have rifles?

THUMMMMP.

The thing in the truck gave a powerful kick.

I don't like this, I decided. I ducked behind a fat tree trunk before they saw me. I pressed against the rough bark and listened to their conversation.

"Why are we catching these things?" the bald one said.

"Beats me. Maybe the boss is starting a zoo," his partner replied.

I held my breath, listening.

"Finish eating," the fat one said. "We've got to get this thing out of here before he kicks a hole in the trailer."

"If anyone sees us, it'll be a little hard to explain," his partner agreed.

"Hey, you'd look good in prison gray!" the other one said, laughing.

Prison! They were doing something illegal.

They climbed to their feet.

Please open the trailer, I thought. Open it so I can see what's inside. I peeked out from behind the tree to watch them.

They didn't open the trailer. They picked up their rifles and tossed them into the Jeep. Then they climbed inside and drove away.

I waited until they were out of sight. Then I took off for home.

My mind whirled with everything that I had seen in the woods these past few days. The birds, the bats, the ugly finger, the flickering lights—and now these men.

The lights must have come from the truck. That much I could figure out. And the men could have upset the bats and the birds.

I've got to talk to Dad, I thought. I've got to tell him about those men and the rifles.

I ran all the way to the backyard. I started shouting halfway across the lawn. "Dad? Are you home? Dad?"

I charged into the house.

"Dad?"

No reply.

No note on the fridge.

I wheeled around and tore back outside to the shed. I pounded on the door with my fist. "Dad? It's me! Open up!"

Silence.

"Dad?"

I grabbed the door handle and started to pull.

"Oh!" I let out a gasp when I heard a loud *click*. Right over my head.

I looked up—and stared at a camera. A little black camera over the door. The kind of security camera they have in banks and stores.

It clicked again.

This is sick, I thought. So sick. I can't believe my dad put a camera up there. He has totally lost it.

I forced back a sob and backed away from the shed door.

I can't take this anymore, I thought. I have to see what's inside.

I ran back to the house. I found the key in the little

cup in the kitchen and carried it outside.

I stopped at the shed door.

Should I really do this? The key shook in my trembling hand. I backed away from the door.

Click.

A wave of disgust washed over me as the camera took my picture again and again.

I pulled open the padlock. Took a deep breath.

And stepped inside the shed.

"Whew!" The sharp aroma of alcohol and other chemicals stung my nostrils. I clicked on the ceiling light. And glanced around.

Where were the animals? The back wall had metal cages stacked to the ceiling. But the cages were all empty, most of the doors hanging open.

I crossed to the worktable. One side was cluttered with jars and bottles. An endless, clear tube, filled with a bright red liquid, snaked like a Crazy Straw over the table and emptied into a large bottle.

Hypodermic needles lay scattered on the rest of the table. Long ones and short ones. Some empty. Others filled with a pink fluid.

An electrical generator hummed quietly in one corner. Metal dishes were stacked on top of it. An open tool kit bulged with wrenches and pliers. Next to that stood my father's desk, and behind it, cartons of books and papers, stacked three high, against the wall.

My eyes darted from one side of the room to the other. Nothing unusual here.

I walked over to the desk and saw a blue binder in the center. A desk lamp was aimed down at it. I leaned over the desk and studied the binder.

Did this have Dad's secret in it? Was this the record of what Dad was working on?

My hand trembled as I opened it. The pages were filled with typed formulas in blue and red ink.

After a long paragraph the word FAILURE had been typed in large letters. After another long paragraph the word DIED had been typed in red.

"The animals don't respond." This was underlined on the next page.

And then I read these chilling words: *"If we kill them, we will learn more. How many can we kill?"*

"Oooh," I moaned. Those words made me feel dizzy.

Dad was killing animals. This was too much. It was too much for me to handle.

I backed out of the shed. I closed the door and snapped the lock.

"I have to get away from here," I said out loud.

I had to go somewhere quiet and peaceful. Somewhere I could think.

A hummingbird buzzed above a tall reed that swayed over the pond. I raised my camera to my eye. The hummingbird darted to the water.

Click. I snapped the shutter. Then I lowered the camera around my neck and watched the hummingbird flit across the water.

Clouds drifted over the lowering sun, casting deep evening shadows through the trees. Every few minutes I felt cold raindrops on my head and shoulders.

But I didn't care. I *had* to come to the woods. I had to be here, where I felt at home. At peace. In the gentle quiet, surrounded by trees, the water shimmering darkly in front of me, I could catch my breath and think.

I turned and saw the tall, fat fern leaves shake on the other side of the pond. Must be an animal in there, I decided. I raised my camera. Come on, I silently urged. Show yourself. I need to finish my project.

I held my breath as a raccoon poked out from the fern leaves. Yes!

I didn't wait for him to come all the way to the water. I clicked once. Twice.

Gotcha.

My mood started to lift.

But then I heard voices behind me, from the other side of the path. And a loud *thunk thunk.*

The raccoon darted away. I spun around. Took a few steps toward the sounds. And saw the camouflaged Jeep and its trailer.

The two men walked along the path up ahead of

the trailer. Their rifles rested against their shoulders.

I placed my hands around my camera. Then slowly raised it to my face.

I'll take a few pictures of them, I decided. And show them to Dr. Carpenter.

I stepped out onto the path. Aimed it at the two men. And clicked off two quick shots.

The snap of the shutter echoed in the quiet woods.

The men spun around quickly. One of them pointed. "Hey—!" he called.

I knew I couldn't outrun them. I had to talk to them. "Hi," I said, trying to sound calm. "What's going on?" I motioned to the Jeep and trailer.

Thunk thunk thunnnnnk.

The men glanced at one another and didn't answer.

The fat one tugged at his cap and studied me. "You live around here? How come you're in the woods?" he asked. He had a hoarse, raspy voice, as if he had a sore throat or maybe smoked too much.

"It's not a good time to be in the woods," his partner said coldly. He had silvery gray eyes that reminded me of ice.

"I'm . . . working on a science project," I said. My hand trembled as I raised the camera to show them.

They both glared at the camera. "What are you taking pictures of?" the bald one asked.

"Plants and animals," I replied.

Thummmp thunnk.

"What kind of animals?" the bald one asked, frowning.

"Animals that use the pond," I said. "You know. Chipmunks . . . rabbits . . . raccoons . . . "

They both nodded.

I stared at the rifles on their shoulders. They knew what I was looking at, but they didn't say anything.

"You explore the woods a lot?" the one in the baseball cap asked finally.

I nodded. "Yeah. Sometimes."

"See anything strange?" he asked.

"No. Not really," I replied. I was dying to ask them what they were doing. And what they had in the trailer.

But before I could get the question out, they raised their rifles to their waists. And then they came at me, eyes so cold, expressions so hard.

Gripping their rifles, they moved quickly. Walking heavily toward me.

No chance to run.

"What—what are you going to do?" I whispered.

"You'd better give us the camera," the bald one said, narrowing his eyes at me.

"Excuse me?" I gaped at him.

"We'd better have that film," he said. "If you don't mind."

"I *do* mind!" I cried.

But his partner moved fast. He grabbed the camera and tugged it off my neck.

"Hey—give me that!" I shouted. "I need that! That's mine!" I made a grab for it—and missed.

He snapped open the camera and pulled out the film cartridge. He yanked the film from the cartridge, exposing it to the sunlight. Ruining it.

Then he handed the camera back.

"You have no right to do that." I scowled angrily.

They turned and walked to the Jeep, carrying their rifles at their waists.

"What's in the trailer?" I shouted. "What's kicking so hard in there?"

They exchanged glances. The bald one swung his rifle onto his shoulder.

"It's a deer," his partner said.

"Yeah, it's a deer," the bald one repeated, his silvery eyes flashing. "We've got a sick deer in there."

"But—the rifles—" I blurted out.

"Tranquilizer guns," the one in the cap said.

"We're taking this deer to be treated," the bald one said. "He's in pretty bad shape. Something bad going on here."

"You should stay out of the woods for a while," his partner warned. "Yeah. And don't take pictures. It's dangerous."

Was he threatening me?

I watched them climb into the Jeep. The bald one started the engine. The Jeep roared and sent a cloud of black exhaust up to the treetops. Then it rumbled away, the trailer bouncing heavily behind it.

I stood in the path, waiting to calm down. I clenched and unclenched my fists at my sides.

"Those two creeps are liars," I said out loud.

That wasn't a sick deer in that trailer. How could a sick deer kick that hard if it was tranquilized?

Those men were definitely lying.

I jumped over a jagged, white rock and started along the path to home. I had walked only a few steps when I saw a little creature, half-hidden by a thick tuft of grass.

It looked like a newborn pig. It had tiny, round

black eyes and a cute pink snout.

It can't be a baby pig, I thought. There aren't any pigs in these woods. I leaned down to get a closer look. Are you a wild pig? You must be some kind of runt!

The little creature let out a squeak—and jumped into my hand.

I cried out in surprise. I nearly dropped it.

It sat in my palm, staring up at me with those cute, little black eyes.

"Wow. You're a friendly guy," I said to it. I raised my palm to study it. "I'm glad you're not afraid of me. I wish I had something to feed you."

It tilted its round head to one side, as if it understood me. It squeaked again, twitched its pink snout, and opened its mouth. I was startled to see two rows of sharp, pointed teeth.

I really have to photograph this guy, I thought. But I don't have any film. I think I'll bring him home with me and take his picture there.

He jumped again. Onto my shoulder.

A second later I felt a sharp stab of pain in my neck.

"Owwww!" I uttered a shocked cry as the creature clamped its teeth into my throat.

"Hey—OWWWW!" I gripped its back and struggled to pull it off me.

But the pain made me stop.

The pain . . . the pain . . .

It shot down my whole body.

The teeth were so deep—and shut so tightly—if I pulled the creature away, I'd tear a hole in my throat!

"Noooo!" I moaned, gripping the animal, squeezing it, struggling to remove it.

Warm liquid trickled down my neck. My blood!

I heard a lapping sound. Sucking and lapping.

The pain throbbed and pulsed.

The blood flowed down my neck.

The pointed teeth chomped and dug in hard.

The lapping and smacking sounds grew more rapid. Frantic.

He's drinking . . . I realized.

Drinking my blood.

Gripping the tiny pig, I could feel it start to swell up. Its belly inflated, and I could feel liquid sloshing around inside.

My blood!

I opened my mouth in a scream of horror. "NOOOOOOO!"

The creature drank furiously, sucking hard, its teeth cutting my skin.

I screamed again. Again.

I dropped to my knees. I started to feel weak . . . so weak.

And then I heard a shout. The snap of twigs.

Dad stepped out from the trees, his eyes wild, his face twisted in fear.

He spotted me down on the ground. And then his mouth dropped open in surprise as he saw the creature at my throat.

"Hold still! Hold still!" he screamed.

He dived down beside me. Dropped to the

ground. Reached both hands for the creature.

"Don't pull it!" I shrieked. "It'll rip a hole—"

Dad clenched his teeth as he struggled to pry the little animal's jaws apart. His face darkened to red. "Yessss!" he cried finally.

He stumbled back. I saw the creature leap from his hand and scramble into the tall grass.

The pain still throbbed in my throat. I touched my neck and felt the warm blood trickling down my skin.

"Are you okay? Laura? Are you okay?" Dad kept repeating. He leaned over me and pushed my hand away so he could see the wound.

"I . . . don't know," I whispered.

"Here." Dad pulled a handkerchief from his back pocket and handed it to me. "Press this against your neck. It will stop the bleeding."

I held the handkerchief against my neck, and Dad helped pull me to my feet.

"Whoa," I murmured, shaking my head. I felt dizzy, kind of light-headed. "What happened? What *was* that?"

Dad shook his head. "I didn't really get a good look at it," he said. "I was so busy prying its jaws apart. . . . And then it ran off. How do you feel? Are you okay?"

"Okay, I guess. The pain is starting to fade." I let out a deep breath. "But it was so weird," I said, picturing the little animal jumping into my hand, then lunging for my neck. "It didn't just bite me. It was sucking my blood." I shuddered. "It was sucking my blood like a vampire."

"Let me see your neck." Dad took the wadded-up handkerchief and studied the wound.

"I don't like the way that looks." His brow tightened with worry. "We have to get to Dr. Davis right now."

Dr. Davis took us into his office immediately. He is a short, pudgy, egg-shaped man with a tiny head. He reminds me of an ostrich.

"Laura—what happened?" he asked, leading me to the examining table.

"Something bit her," Dad said. "A baby chipmunk, maybe. But I'm not sure. It was hard to tell because whatever it was, it had lost all its fur."

I stared over the doctor's shoulder at Dad. Why did he lie? No way that was a chipmunk. Why didn't he tell Dr. Davis that it was a strange little pig?

Dr. Davis examined the wound. "It could have been a diseased animal. Maybe rabid," he said softly. "Did it look rabid?" the doctor asked.

"I'm sorry," Dad answered. "It ran off. I just don't know."

"Rabies shots are very painful," Dr. Davis said. "I'll rush your blood sample to the lab before we start with shots. I'll have the results by tomorrow morning at the very latest. In the meantime, I'll give you a prescription for strong antibiotics. Start taking them right away."

Rabies. My stomach tightened. Please let the blood tests be okay, I thought. I watched Dr. Davis prepare a needle and thread to stitch up the wound.

I closed my eyes and pictured the animal that bit me. I saw its pink body. Its little piglike snout. It was not a chipmunk, I thought. It was definitely not a chipmunk.

A short while later Dad and I crossed the parking lot to the car. "How does it look?" I asked. "Do I look like Frankenstein now?"

Dad ran his fingers gently over my neck. "It should heal without much of a scar," he replied. "It might itch after a while. Try not to scratch it, okay?"

"Yeah, sure," I muttered.

"Do you have any symptoms at all?" Dad asked as we reached the car. "Do you feel at all strange or sick?"

I shook my head. "No, I feel okay."

I climbed into the car and waited for him to slide behind the wheel. Dr. Davis had given me some painkillers, but my throat still ached.

"Dad, why did you tell Dr. Davis it was a chipmunk?" I asked. "It didn't look like a chipmunk."

Dad started the engine and backed out of the parking space. "I didn't see it very well. And without its fur, it was hard to tell what it was."

"But it looked like a pig," I said. "It had a snout. It didn't look like chipmunk at all. Why didn't you say it looked like a pig?"

Dad turned to me. "It was simpler, Laura. That's all. It doesn't really matter. We'll get your blood tests and find out what to do next."

I swallowed and stared out the window. We drove for a while in silence. "I hate to say it, but I'm a little afraid to go back in the woods," I confessed.

"Don't worry about that," Dad said. "You won't be back in the woods for a long while."

My mouth dropped open in surprise. "Excuse me? Why not?"

"Why not?" Dad raised his eyebrows. "You're the one seeing vampire pigs! Do *you* think the woods are safe right now?"

"But—but—" I started to protest.

"But what, Laura?" Dad shook his head. "We don't know what bit you. Whatever it was, it could be rabid. And we know it's dangerous. Aren't those enough reasons?"

I could see there was no point in arguing. I turned away from Dad and stared out the window the rest of the way home.

As soon as we reached our house, I ran up to my room and slammed the door. I dropped facedown on my bed and buried my face in the pillow.

I *have* to go into the woods, I thought. He can't keep me out. He can't!

A short while later I heard Dad's voice downstairs. He was talking to someone on the phone. I climbed out of bed and pulled my door open a crack.

"She seems to be fine," he said.

Who was he talking to? Dr. Davis?

"By tomorrow. We'll have the blood tests in the morning," Dad said.

Not Dr. Davis.

I walked to the top of the stairs. I could hear Dad so clearly now. I could hear what he said next—the cruelest, most hurtful words I'd ever heard in my life.

"Can you take Laura for a while? A trip to Chicago right now would help. I really have to get her out of here."

I called Ellen right away. And in a trembling voice begged her to come over.

She and Stevie Palmer had made up, and she was supposed to go biking with him and a couple of other guys. But she said she'd tell them to go without her.

A few minutes later she showed up. I pulled her up to my room. "Laura, what's wrong?" she asked, dropping onto the edge of my bed. "You sounded so weird on the phone."

"It's Dad. He's sending me away!" I cried. "I—I heard him on the phone. With Mom. He asked if Mom could take me. He—he said he had to get me out of here."

Ellen jumped to her feet. "I don't believe it." She shook her head. "He can't send you away just like that. What's wrong with him?"

"I—I don't know," I stammered. "Maybe it was because of the animal that attacked me." I told Ellen about the little pig. Then I showed her my neck.

"Oh, gross." She gasped. "Does it hurt?"

"No, but Dad said I can't go into the woods anymore. He thinks it's too dangerous," I said, running my fingers over the raw stitches. "But then he called Mom and . . . and . . . " A sob burst from my throat.

"How could he do that?" I wailed. "He just wants to get rid of me. He called my mom without even talking to me about it. How could he, Ellen? He doesn't even care about me anymore."

Ellen hurried across the room and hugged me. "Of course he cares about you," she said. "He was upset that you were attacked. He just wants you to be safe. That's why he called your mom. But he's not serious. He'd never send you away."

"He's serious," I insisted. "He's very serious, Ellen. He wants to get rid of me."

I took a deep breath—and a new thought came to me. One that sent a shiver down my spine. "I know why he's doing this. He checked the film in his camera on the shed. He saw that I was in there."

"Whoa. Slow down." Ellen raised a hand. "Your father has a camera on the shed now?"

I nodded.

"And you went inside? What was in there?" she asked.

"His instruments and stuff. That's all," I told her. I didn't want to talk about the journal I had found. I didn't know if my father was killing animals or not. And I didn't want to say anything to Ellen until I was sure.

73

"What about the animals? What about the one we heard howling?" she asked.

"There weren't any animals inside. I don't know what happened to them," I said.

I plopped down on my bed. "I'm not going to Chicago. I'm not!" I declared.

Ellen's chin trembled. "I sure hope not," she said softly. I could see she was really upset, too. But then a smile crossed her face. "At least, not until after my birthday party!"

We both laughed.

She always knows how to make me laugh.

"I have to make him change his mind," I said. "And the only way I can do that is to find out what is making him act so strange. If only—"

I stopped when I heard a sharp cry from outside. We both turned to the open window.

"What was that?" Ellen asked.

A horrifying howl rang out. A shrill cry of pain.

And then I heard a different sound.

An animal screech.

I dived for the window and peered out into the evening darkness.

A hunched figure darted toward the woods. I could see it loping away on four legs. It was about the size of a large dog.

As it reached the edge of the woods, it stopped— and I gasped. It stood up. Stood on two legs—and charged into the trees.

My eyes searched the backyard—
And on the ground . . .
. . . on the ground . . .
Lying on his side on the ground . . .
"Georgie!" I screamed. "Oh, no! Georgie!"

Ellen and I flew out of my bedroom and down the stairs. I pushed open the kitchen door and tore across the grass.

"Georgie! Are you okay?" I cried.

The poor dog lay on his side whimpering. His legs twitched. His chest heaved up and down.

"Georgie? Georgie?"

I dropped beside him. I started to pet his head. His eyes rolled crazily. His tongue fell limply from his mouth.

"Ohhhh. Look. His leg," Ellen moaned. "Ohhhhh. Sick."

I followed her gaze. Georgie's leg . . . oh . . . Georgie's leg . . .

The creature had practically chewed it off.

The fur had been ripped away. Chunks of flesh had been torn off. Blood flowed onto the grass. I could see veins pulsing in the chewed-up mess, and a white bone poked out.

My breath caught in my chest. I couldn't stop myself. I started to gag. I could feel my dinner lurch up to my throat, and I struggled to choke it back.

I forced myself to turn away from the horrifying wound. "Georgie," I whispered, petting his head softly. "You'll be okay. You'll be okay."

The dog whimpered softly, too weak to raise his head from the grass.

I looked up to see Ellen running, bringing my dad, pointing furiously to Georgie. "He was attacked!" I shouted to Dad. "His leg—it's pretty bad."

Dad's mouth dropped open when he saw the chewed-up leg. "He's losing a lot of blood. I'll slow the bleeding." Dad took off his T-shirt and shredded it.

"Laura, go in the house and get the bandages," he said as he wrapped Georgie's leg in a strip from his T-shirt. "We'd better get him to a vet—fast. He's going to need surgery on this leg."

Dad and I carried poor Georgie to the van and set him down gently on the backseat. He stared at us with those big, dark eyes and didn't move. We were covered in blood.

"I'll call you later," I told Ellen. I climbed into the van beside Dad.

"Hope he's okay," Ellen said, shaking her head sadly. Her eyes glistened with tears. "Call me!"

As Dad backed the van down the driveway,

Georgie whimpered softly behind us.

"I think I saw the animal that attacked Georgie," I said.

"What was it?" Dad kept his eyes on the road.

"Well, I'm not really sure. It was too dark to see clearly. But it was about Georgie's size—" I told him.

"Well, that could be anything," Dad interrupted.

"I know," I said. "But here's the weird thing. It was running on four legs. And then it stopped and stood up, and ran into the woods on two legs."

Dad swallowed. "Two legs?" He didn't take his eyes off the road.

"Yes. Isn't that strange?"

Dad didn't reply.

I glanced out the window. Most of the houses we passed were dark. Georgie cried softly in the back-seat.

"Hey, wait!" I cried. "This isn't the way to the animal hospital! Dad—turn around!"

"I'm not going to the animal hospital," Dad said softly, still avoiding my stare.

"But—but—" I sputtered.

"There's a good place in Walker Falls," he said. "I know the doctors there. They will—"

"Walker Falls? But that's two towns away!" I shrieked.

"It's a good place," Dad insisted. "They're experts at this kind of surgery."

"But, Dad—"

Finally he turned to me. To my shock, his eyes were cold. His expression remained hard. "Don't argue with me, Laura. I know what I'm doing."

"Okay. Fine." I sighed. I turned away from him and stared out the window.

We drove the rest of the way in silence.

Dad won't go near the animal hospital, I realized. Even in an emergency like this one.

Why won't he go there? I wondered.

What did he do that he can no longer face Dr. Carpenter?

What horrible thing did he do?

We had to leave Georgie in the hospital. The vet cleaned and stitched up the wound. But he wasn't sure if Georgie's leg could be saved. We'd have to wait and see.

When we got home, I couldn't sleep. I tossed and turned all night, thinking about Georgie, thinking about the weird animal that attacked him. So many strange things were going on in the woods.

I had to find out what was going on there. And I couldn't do it from Chicago.

My whole life suddenly seemed out of control. I was afraid now of the thing I loved most—the woods. And I was angry with Dad. Angry because he didn't trust me. Or confide in me. Angry because he wanted to send me away.

I was afraid of him, too, I realized. I didn't know my own father anymore. I was afraid of what he might do next.

After school I hurried to the animal hospital. Dr.

Carpenter greeted me in the waiting room. She looked really stressed. She had dark rings under her eyes, and her blond hair was unbrushed, falling in damp tangles.

Before I had a chance to say hi, she spotted the wound on my throat. "Laura, what happened? Did Georgie bite you?"

"No. I—I was bitten by a—" I didn't know what to say. I didn't know what had bitten me.

"What was it?" Dr. Carpenter asked.

"Well, it looked like a little pig. With really sharp teeth." I let out a nervous laugh. "I know it sounds crazy. . . . "

"Where was this little pig?" Dr. Carpenter asked. "Where were you when you got bitten?"

"In the woods," I told her.

"A little pig with sharp teeth running around in the woods. It does sound crazy, doesn't it?" Dr. Carpenter frowned. "What does your dad think?"

I let out a sigh. "I don't know. He told Dr. Davis it was a chipmunk. He just said that because it was simpler than trying to explain what it really looked like."

"Oh. Did your Dad see it, too?" she asked.

"I think so," I answered.

Dr. Carpenter leaned close to me and studied the wound carefully. She smoothed her fingers gently around the stitches. "That's nasty," she muttered. She raised her eyes to me. "Did your doctor give you a rabies shot? Or any kind of antibiotic?"

"We got my blood test results this morning. I don't need a rabies shot," I said. "He did give me antibiotics." And then I gasped. "Oh, no. Dad picked up the pills. But he forgot to give them to me."

Dr. Carpenter put her arm around my shoulder. "Don't worry. The wound doesn't look infected. But it is a little swollen. I think I should give you an injection to stop the swelling."

I had forgotten that Dr. Carpenter was a medical doctor as well as a vet. "Okay, but I guess I should check with my dad first," I said.

"Tell you what," Dr. Carpenter said. "I'll call your dad right now and ask his permission. Okay?"

"Well . . . yeah," I replied. "Thank you, Dr. Carpenter."

She disappeared for a few minutes, leaving me in the waiting room. When she returned, she had a smile on her face. "He apologized for forgetting the pills, Laura. He said it would be a good idea to give you the injection right away."

"Okay. Great," I said. I was trying to sound brave. I *hate* shots!

She led the way into the lab. Then she pulled some bottles from a cabinet and prepared the injection.

"How . . . how did my dad sound when you spoke to him?" I asked her.

"Fine." She glanced up at me. "Well, maybe a little

tired. Why? Is he not feeling well?"

"No. No. He's okay. Sort of," I said.

"Is he still upset about leaving the animal hospital?" she asked.

"I—I don't think that's it," I said.

"What is it, Laura? What's troubling you?" Dr. Carpenter sat down on a stool beside me.

"I have a feeling something happened here before Dad left. Something bad." I let out a deep breath.

"Something bad?" Dr. Carpenter asked. "What would make you think that?"

I didn't want to tell her about Georgie. If I told her that Dad refused to come here, she'd feel terrible.

But I didn't have a choice.

"Georgie was attacked the other night and Dad took him to Walker Falls. He wouldn't come here," I said in a rush.

Dr. Carpenter didn't say anything. She just nodded.

"Do you know why he wouldn't come here?" I asked.

She didn't answer. Instead, she stood up, rubbed alcohol on my arm with a wad of cotton, and raised the needle.

"OUCH!" I tried not to scream as the needle punctured my skin. But I couldn't hold it in.

Dr. Carpenter frowned. "That wasn't so bad, was it?" She dabbed cotton on it. "It should help the swelling."

Then she gave me a green pill, an antibiotic, to

take. She placed the rest of the pills in a small plastic bottle and handed it to me. "Be sure to take a pill every morning."

I clutched the vial in my hand. "But—what were you going to say about my dad?" I asked.

She sighed. "Laura, if your dad doesn't want to talk about what happened, it's not my place to tell you. I think he has to be the one."

She straightened her lab coat. "Why don't you come back tomorrow? I'll check your stitches, and we can talk some more then."

"Okay," I said. I started to the door. "Thanks."

"Laura—" Dr. Carpenter called after me. "Maybe you should stay out of the woods for a while."

I stared at her. She was saying the same thing as Dad!

No way, I thought. No way am I staying out of the woods.

I had too many questions.

And no answers.

The next afternoon I sat in my backyard doing my homework. I leaned against a tree, reading my English textbook. I never mind homework if I can sit outside and do it.

"Hey! What's up?" Joe walked across the grass toward me.

"Hi!" I dropped my book onto the grass and smiled. Joe was wearing black jeans and a gray T-shirt, and he looked really cute!

"How's your dog?" he asked.

"Still in the hospital," I said, standing up. "The vet operated on him last night. We won't know for a while if he can keep the leg or not."

Joe's eyes bulged with surprise. "Huh? Your dog is in the hospital?"

"Isn't that why you asked?" I said.

He shook his head. "The last time I saw you, your dog nearly attacked you. Remember?"

"Oh, right." So much had happened since then. I told Joe about the horrible attack on Georgie.

Joe gasped. "You mean . . . they might cut the leg off?" He twisted a knot of his long hair between his fingers. "I'm sorry," he muttered. "That's such bad news."

"I know," I said. "But here's some good news." I took a deep breath. "I'm throwing a birthday party on Saturday for my friend Ellen. Can you come?"

There. I finally said it.

Joe hesitated for a moment. "Yeah, sure," he said. "Cool."

Wait till I tell Ellen he's coming to the party! I thought. This is awesome!

"Why don't you get your camera?" he said. "Let's take a walk to the pond."

"Great!" A few seconds later Joe and I were heading to the pond.

At first I felt nervous walking in the woods. But

we didn't see anything unusual, and it was really nice spending time with Joe.

We sat by the pond and talked and talked. I didn't see any animals to photograph, but I really wasn't paying attention. Before I knew it, it was close to dinnertime.

"See you Saturday." Joe stood up and started away, then turned back. "Hope your dog comes home soon."

"Thanks," I said. I watched him walk away, pushing tall weeds out of his path.

I should have asked him where *he* lives, I thought. I'll have to remember for next time.

Then I had an idea. I'll follow him home, I decided.

I turned and trotted along the path. I could hear Joe's crunching footsteps a little up ahead.

I slowed to a walk. I didn't want him to catch me following him. That would be *so* not cool.

The path curved and Joe came into view. He was walking rapidly, tapping a long stick he had picked up on the tree trunks he passed.

The path led beneath leafy old trees that bent low over the ground. The thick leaves blocked the afternoon sunlight and made the woods as dark as evening.

I kept far behind Joe, squinting into the dim light. He was jogging now, moving quickly through the deepening shadows.

I came out at the end of the trees, but I had lost him.

I gazed down the path. No sign of him. I turned and swept my eyes along the grassy clearing to my right. No. No Joe.

A rock wall stood to my left. It was as tall as me. Had he climbed over it? Where had he gone?

"I give up," I muttered. I turned and started back toward the pond. But I stopped just short of the trees when I spotted something in the clearing.

I took a few steps closer. And realized it was some kind of shack. A small, homemade hut, no bigger than a camping tent.

"Hey—is anyone in there?" I called.

No reply.

I made my way through the tall grass and stepped up to it. The walls were constructed of evergreen branches clumped together and tied with rope and bits of string. Sticks and fat leaves had been used to fill in holes the branches didn't cover.

"Anyone in there?" I called, softer this time.

Silence.

I leaned forward and poked my head through the opening in the leafy wall. It was dark inside, but circles of sunshine washed in from the top.

My eyes stopped on one of the circles of light—and I froze. And stared.

Stared at two hairy, leathery fingers on the hut floor.

And beside them . . . beside them . . . a small pile of bones . . . animal bones. Most of them had been picked clean. But some still had chunks of meat and fur clinging to them.

And in the corner . . . piled up in the corner, I saw animal heads. Even in the dim light, I could see them so clearly. Piled on top of each other. Rabbit heads, squirrel heads, a couple of raccoon heads, eyes staring blankly, glassily at me.

"NOOOO!" I screamed without realizing it.

What kind of creature lives here? What kind of beast builds its own hut and keeps dead animals inside it?

The whole shack trembled as I pulled my head out. I spun away. The animal bones, the heads, the milky eyes lingered in my mind.

I spun away and ran. Ran across the clearing. I was halfway to the trees when I heard the roar behind me.

The roar of an engine.

I swung around—and saw the camouflaged Jeep racing across the clearing toward me, the trailer bouncing hard behind it.

"STOP!" I screamed, waving my hands.

But the Jeep picked up speed.

"STOP!" I turned and started to run.

The engine roared. The Jeep plowed over small trees and weeds as it sped after me. Behind it the trailer rocked from side to side, so hard I thought it might flip over.

They want to run me down! I realized. They're not going to stop!

I leaped over a boulder and kept running. But the Jeep was catching up. I crossed the path, lowered my head, and ran.

I didn't remember the stone wall until it was too late.

No time to climb it. No time to run to the side.

I was trapped. Trapped against the wall.

I spun around and watched the Jeep race toward me.

I'm going to be crushed, I realized. I shut my eyes, gritted my teeth, and tensed all my muscles.

And heard the scrape of tires as the Jeep went into a wild spin.

I opened my eyes to see that it had stopped inches in front of me. I stared as the driver stuck his head out the window.

He stuck his head out—and I recognized him. And gasped. "Oh, noooo. You! It's YOU!"

I didn't believe it. How could this be?

"Dad!" I cried. "Wh-what are you doing in there?"

I ran up to the side of the Jeep. "Dad? What are you doing here?" I cried.

His glasses glinted in the afternoon sunlight. I couldn't see his eyes. He scowled at me. His face was bright red.

"Get in," he growled.

"Dad—answer my question," I said.

"Get in," he repeated angrily. "I told you to stay out of the woods."

I stared at him. His expression was so cold, so angry, I barely recognized him.

"I'm taking you home," he said. "Get in the Jeep—now."

"N-not until you explain," I insisted. "What have you got in the trailer? What are you *doing* here, Dad?"

He uttered another growl. Then he shoved open the Jeep door and jumped out.

He grabbed my arm and started to pull me. "Get

in, Laura. I don't have time for this."

"Ow! You're *hurting* me!" I cried. I tried to pull free.

He tightened his grip. And dragged me around to the other side of the Jeep.

He has totally changed, I thought. He isn't the same person. He has turned into some kind of *monster*!

He forced me into the passenger seat and slammed the door.

My whole body trembled. I hugged myself to stop the shaking.

How can this be? I thought. I'm terrified. Terrified of my own father. . . .

The week passed slowly. I didn't feel very well. I felt tired and weak, as if I had the flu. The wound on my neck ached and throbbed.

Dad didn't mention sending me off to Mom again. My stomach felt twisted in knots as I waited for him to say something about it. But he never brought it up.

I was really looking forward to Ellen's birthday party, and I spent the week planning it. I wanted it to be a lot of fun—for Ellen and for me, too. I needed something to cheer me up.

I woke up Saturday, the day of the party, and ran to the window. Yes! The weather was going to be great. It was a sunny, warm day. The air smelled fresh and sweet. The green trees of the woods glowed like emeralds. It was the perfect day for a party.

Blue is Ellen's favorite color. So after breakfast I ran outside and covered the backyard with blue streamers and dozens of blue balloons. I hauled our picnic table to the center of the lawn and covered it with a blue tablecloth.

I even had blue icing on Ellen's birthday cake!

When Ellen arrived, she couldn't believe the backyard. "It's awesome, Laura. Awesome!" she declared. She gave me a hug, then hurried off to talk to two boys who had just arrived.

Up to the last minute Ellen had kept adding people to the guest list, then changing her mind and cutting them off.

Finally I just invited everyone from our class.

I cranked up the portable CD player and brought out trays of pizza. About twenty kids had shown up. They were laughing and kidding around and eating.

Ellen, surrounded by boys, flashed me a thumbs-up. I could see she was enjoying the party.

Where is Joe? I wondered. I kept waiting for him to arrive. I was dying for Ellen to meet him.

I checked to make sure there were enough Cokes. Then I brushed some flies away from the birthday cake.

When I looked up from the food table, I saw Dad crossing the lawn, making his way into the shed. His expression was glum. He kept his head down and didn't seem to notice the kids or the party.

"Dad—do you want some pizza?" I called.

He waved his hand, signaling no. Then he disappeared into the shed, quickly closing the door behind him.

I turned back to the party. I didn't want to think about Dad now.

Yes, he had given me permission to have the party in the backyard. "Just make sure no one goes into the woods," he said sternly. "I mean it, Laura. No one."

I sighed, remembering my birthday parties when I was little. We always had a scavenger hunt in the woods. Dad always set them up. He would hide things up in trees and under rocks, and sometimes even floating in the stream.

Dad was a lot of fun in those days, I thought.

I gazed sadly at the shed. Then, shaking away my unhappy thoughts, I turned back to the party.

"Time to cut the cake, everyone!" I shouted over the music. "Hey—who wants birthday cake?"

A few kids wandered toward the food table. Some girls were dancing in the middle of the yard. A bunch of guys were tossing a Frisbee around.

"Hey, Ellen—come cut your cake!" I shouted. I searched the yard for her. "Has anyone seen Ellen?" I asked.

A few kids looked around, trying to help me find her.

"She went off with Stevie," a boy called.

"Huh? Where?" I asked.

The boy pointed to the trees. "I saw them heading into the woods."

"Oh, no," I moaned. If Dad found out that kids went into the woods, he would stop the party!

I had to bring them back—fast.

I took off running across the backyard. "I'll be right back!" I called. I made my way onto the path and started to shout as I entered the woods. "Ellen? Hey, Ellen? Stevie?"

No reply.

I followed the path through a growth of tall weeds, over a fallen log. "Ellen? Stevie? Where are you guys?"

I walked all the way to the pond, then turned around.

How could she do this to me? I asked myself angrily. Doesn't she know how much trouble she's getting me into?

I wandered in circles, calling out their names. I became angrier and angrier as I walked.

"Stevie? Ellen?" I called. My eyes searched the trees. "Are you here?"

No reply.

A bird cawed. An ugly, raw sound, as if it had something stuck in its throat.

"Hey—if you're hiding, it isn't funny!" I yelled.

I heard footsteps. Fast, running footsteps through the trees behind me.

I spun around. "Ellen? Stevie? Is that you?"

"Hunnh hunnh." Animal grunts. Very close by.

I froze. My breath caught in my throat.

"Hunnnnh." A long, low grunt.

And then a high, shrill squeal. A horrible, frightening cry—like an animal in pain.

I ran toward the sound.

My heart pounding, I raced from tree to tree, searching frantically, frightened of what I'd find.

In front of me I saw a clump of evergreen shrubs shaking. A flash of red through the greenery. Then I heard a long, loud *ripping* sound. It reminded me of a Velcro shoe being torn open.

My heart skipped a beat as I moved closer to the shrubs.

I heard a moan, soft and weak.

And then I stopped when I heard the chewing. The crack of bone breaking.

Loud chewing . . . chewing . . . chewing . . .

I couldn't stand it anymore.

I had to see what was on the other side of the shrub.

With a pounding heart, I moved around the bushes, looked down at the ground—and opened my mouth in an endless scream.

A deer was sprawled on its side in the tall grass. Its head had been torn off. The head sat straight up a few feet from the body. One eye stared blankly at me. The other eye had been yanked out.

The body had been clawed apart. Pale white bones and bright red meat poked out through the torn fur. A swarm of flies already buzzed around the opening.

"It . . . it's half-eaten," I choked out.

I stared in horror at the deer. Most of the insides had been ripped out and devoured. The fur sagged loosely, like an empty bag.

"Oh, sick," I moaned, finally turning away. "Sick."

What kind of animal did this? There were no bears in these woods. So what was big enough and strong enough—and *hungry* enough—to do this?

And what if the deer hadn't come along? I thought.

I was so close to it. Would the animal have found *me* instead? Would it have ripped me apart and devoured me?

My whole body twisted in a violent shudder. I spun away from the dead deer. And realized that Ellen and Stevie were still out here. I had to find them. I had to make sure they were okay.

I circled back around the evergreen shrubs and found a path that curved towards the pond.

I started to follow the path when I heard the sound of footsteps again. With a frightened cry, I whirled around—and saw a man coming toward me, running fast. Eyeglasses glinted in the light.

"Dad!" I shouted. "Dad—what are you—"

I didn't finish my question.

As he drew closer, I gaped in horror at him. At the red stains all down the front of his clothes.

The red . . . the bright, wet red . . .

My dad—he . . . he was covered in blood.

"The blood," I muttered.

I took a step back, my whole body tight with fear.

My dad stood hunched in front of me, breathing hard. "You promised, Laura. You promised to stay in the backyard."

"But, Dad—" I pointed. "The blood . . . What is that blood?"

He looked down, as if seeing it for the first time. He stared at it for a long moment. "I heard you screaming," he said finally. "I . . . I dropped everything and ran."

The blood stained both of his hands. I saw a patch of it darkening on his chin.

"I ran into a sharp tree branch," he said. "I . . . cut my chest, I guess. I didn't stop to check. I thought you were in trouble."

We stared at each other. I couldn't take my eyes off the bright, red blood. Still wet. Still so wet.

Did I believe his story?

I wanted to believe it. I really did. But I remembered the journal in the shed. *If we kill them, we will learn more. How many can we kill?*

Did Dad kill the deer?

No . . . no . . . please—no!

He pulled off his glasses and wiped them on the side of his pants. He squinted at me. "Are you okay? The screaming . . . are you hurt?"

I shook my head. "No. A deer. I heard a deer being attacked. By some kind of animal. It scared me."

I stared at my father. He couldn't have done it. He couldn't have ripped the deer's head off like that. He couldn't have, I told myself. No way. No way. No way.

Ellen and Stevie and all the other kids were waiting for me when Dad and I returned to the backyard. Dad slipped into the house while everyone gathered around me, talking all at once, smiling, relieved.

"Laura, where did you go?" Ellen asked. "We heard you screaming and—we were so scared."

"Where did *you* go?" I demanded. "I went looking for you—"

"Stevie and I were in the garage," Ellen said. "We were looking for another Frisbee."

"Someone told me you were in the woods," I said, sighing.

"Can we cut the cake now?" a boy shouted.

Everybody laughed.

We cut the birthday cake. It was a little melted and soggy from being left outside for so long.

The party broke up early. No one was really in the mood anymore.

"I'm really sorry," I apologized to Ellen for the hundredth time as she headed away with Stevie and two other guys. "I—I shouldn't have run into the woods like that."

Ellen hugged me. "It was a great party anyway. Oh, I forgot to tell you. Joe was here."

"Huh? When?"

"He showed up right after you went into the woods. But you weren't here, so he left. He's not bad. Kind of shy. But not bad."

I was so disappointed. Why didn't he stay? Oh, well. At least Ellen had finally met him.

After Ellen and the others left, I picked up some dirty paper plates and cups and carried them into the house.

But I couldn't finish cleaning up. I was too upset. And too confused. Dr. Carpenter said I could come back and talk some more—and that's exactly what I was going to do.

Dr. Carpenter knew something about Dad. Something she didn't want to tell me. But I had to make her tell me. I had to know.

I ran out the back door, letting the screen door slam behind me. Then I jumped on my bike and began pedaling hard, heading to the animal hospital.

I hoped she would be there. I really needed her help.

A few minutes later I jumped off my bike, letting it fall to the grass. Then I ran inside the building.

No one at the reception desk. I heard a radio playing down the hall. A few dogs were barking.

"Anyone here?" I called.

No answer. So I made my way to the main office. I pulled open the door. "Dr. Carpenter?" The lights were all on. I saw a cup of coffee and a half-eaten muffin on her desk. But no sign of her.

I'm not leaving this place without answers, I told myself. I can't live with all these questions about Dad. I'm afraid of him now. I can't be afraid of my own father.

I crossed the room to the wall of file cabinets.

I glanced back at the door. No sign of Dr. Carpenter.

I hurried to the file drawers. After a few seconds I found a drawer marked EMPLOYMENT RECORDS.

Yes! I thought. I pulled it out. The drawer was stuffed full. My hand shook as I started to shuffle through the files, searching for the one about my dad.

Finally I found one with his name on it. I lifted it out—and opened it.

Empty. The file was completely empty.

Someone had removed all of his records.

The file folder fell from my hand. I bent to pick it up.

And heard a startled voice from the doorway. "Laura! What are you doing?"

I jumped to my feet. "Dr. Carpenter!" I gasped. "I—I'm so sorry."

Her blond hair gleamed under the ceiling lights. Her green eyes narrowed, studying me. "What are you doing here, Laura? What are you looking for?"

I didn't hold back. I told her everything I was worried about.

I told her about Dad locking himself in the shed day after day. I told her about the camera over the shed door. And about the strange howls and animal cries from inside the shed. I told her about the blood. I told her I thought Dad might be killing animals.

"I—I'm so worried about him, Dr. Carpenter," I said, unable to keep my voice from trembling. "I'm worried. And I'm *afraid* of him. And . . . and he wants to send me away. Can you believe it? *Can you believe he'd actually send me away?*"

She stared at me. "Wow," she muttered. "How awful. I don't believe it, Laura. I really don't. Your father is a good man, even if he . . . "

"Even if what? What is he doing?" I cried. "Do you know? Why did he leave his job here? You have to tell me! You *have* to!"

She sighed and settled into her desk chair. She motioned for me to sit across from her. "Okay. Since you're so upset, I'll tell you what happened," she said finally. "But it isn't a happy story, Laura."

I sat stiffly with my hands cold and wet, clamped tightly together in my lap. And I listened to Dr. Carpenter's story. . . .

"Your father and I were working together on some important genetic research with animals. But I began to feel that your dad was going too far. He became obsessed. He worked on the research day and night. And after a while he wouldn't tell me things he was working on. He had a lot of secrets.

"I began to suspect that he was taking the work in a different direction. I thought maybe he was doing experiments that were cruel to the animals."

I listened carefully, trying to understand what Dr. Carpenter was telling me. "What kind of research was he doing?" I asked. "What was he trying to find out?"

"We were trying to understand how genes could be used to fight viruses. By studying the genetic patterns of the animals, we hoped to change the genes and prevent disease—not only in animals, but in people, too. Do you understand what I'm saying?" she asked.

"I think so." I nodded. "And if animals had genes that could fight viruses, then you could figure out how to create virus-fighting genes in humans," I reasoned.

"Exactly!" Dr. Carpenter exclaimed. "It would be so exciting. A medical miracle!"

She sat back in her chair. "But your father started taking the research too far. I heard horrible howls coming from his lab. He wouldn't tell me what he was doing. It was all too disturbing." She let out a deep sigh.

"Your dad and I fought about it," she continued. "We talked about him leaving, but he promised to stop.

"Then one day I was looking for some of my research notes, and they were missing. No one knew where I kept my notes. No one but your dad.

"It was terrible. How could I work with someone I couldn't trust? So I had to ask your dad to leave. It was very sad. But I had no choice."

My mind spinning, I closed my eyes to think about everything Dr. Carpenter had said. And I pictured that little, whimpering animal in the shed. The one he was injecting with the big needle.

I could see my dad plunging the big needle into the squealing animal. And I knew it was all true. . . .

I jumped up. Spun away. And ran out of the room. Out of the animal hospital. I don't even remember if I thanked Dr. Carpenter or said goodbye or anything.

I grabbed my bike and tore out of there, the horrible thoughts raging in my head, whirling like a hurricane. Into the woods. I spent an hour or so wandering among the trees. It had always calmed me to be here. But not this time.

I didn't get home till long after dinnertime. Dad was locked in his shed. I was glad. I didn't want to face him.

I wasn't hungry, but I made a sandwich and took it up to my room. I picked up the phone a couple of times to call Ellen. But each time I changed my mind.

What could I say?

I went to bed a little after eleven and fell into a dreamless sleep. I was awakened a few hours later by a long animal howl. From outside.

I sat up, rubbing my eyes, tugging my sweaty hair off the back of my neck. I climbed out of bed and made my way to the window as another long, sad howl—a howl of pain—floated up from the woods.

Wisps of black cloud snaked over the moon. The trees bent and swayed in a strong breeze.

What is going on out there? I asked myself.

I dressed quickly. Grabbed a flashlight. And tiptoed down the hall. I heard Dad snoring lightly as I passed his room.

I glanced at the kitchen clock as I headed to the back door. Nearly three A.M.

Beaming the flashlight on the ground ahead of me, I crossed the back lawn and stepped into the woods. The moon kept appearing and then disappearing behind the rolling wisps of cloud. A heavy dew made everything sparkle like silver.

OWWWOOOOOOOOOOOO.

I turned at the sound of the howl, my light sweeping over the trees. I stepped off the path and made my way toward the sound.

OWOOOOOOO.

So close. The sound was so close now.

The back of my neck prickled. I suddenly felt cold all over. My hand trembled, and I nearly dropped the flashlight.

I heard a door slam. I swept my light through the trees. It washed over the Jeep and trailer.

I sucked in my breath. Forced myself to stop shaking. I moved in closer.

Hiding behind a tree, I stole a glance into the driver's window. No one there. The Jeep was empty.

I heard a heavy *thud*, followed by another long, mournful howl. From inside the trailer.

I stepped closer, moving the light from side to side.

No one around.

The men must be out hunting other animals, I figured.

What did they have in there? It definitely wasn't a deer.

I'm going to find out, I decided. I'm not leaving until I finally find out.

OWOOOOOO.

The howl grew even louder, more desperate. Did the creature know someone was out here?

My light swept over the back of the trailer until I found a long, silvery bolt on the back door.

I took a deep breath. Lowered the light. Reached for the bolt and tugged it hard.

It slid up easily, and the back doors began to swing open.

OWOOOOOOO.

The long, sad howl greeted me, along with a sour smell.

I raised the light. Aimed it into the trailer, focusing on the animal tied up, sitting on the floor.

I opened my mouth to scream—but no sound came out.

Was it an animal? *Was* it a real, living creature?

"Ohhhhhh." A horrified moan escaped my throat. The flashlight jiggled in my hand. I gripped it in two hands to hold it steady.

And stared . . .

Stared in shock and amazement at the ugly creature gazing back at me. Its body was huge, and piglike. But it had human arms and legs. Its skin was creamy colored but lined and leathery.

And its face . . .

I raised the flashlight, and the light trembled over its face. Its face . . . so ugly . . . so strange. . . .

A pig's face. Round and bald. A snout and two long teeth curling out over its chin. Pointed pig ears. But its eyes—they were human eyes . . . and they looked so sad.

It opened its snout and howled again. It pulled and strained against the thick ropes that held it down.

Staring at me with those sad, watery eyes as if pleading, it shoved its massive body against the wall of the trailer.

Shoved it again. Again. Its fat body shook like Jell-O.

"No," I whispered. "No."

I lowered the light and backed away. I reached for the door handle. I trained my light on the creature for one more look. I shuddered.

Part pig. Part human. Did my father create this beast? Is this what he was doing in secret?

Dr. Carpenter had told the truth, I realized. Dad was doing his own research. His own terrifying experiments.

I shoved the door shut. I was reaching for the bolt when I heard voices.

I spun around and saw two men step out of the trees. The same men I had met before.

Circles of light swept the ground in front of them. Then they both raised their lights to my face. They uttered angry, surprised cries.

I raised my hands to shield my eyes.

"Did she see it? Did she?" the bald one asked.

"Yes," his partner replied.

The bald one let out a low growl. "Grab her," he ordered. "Don't let her get away."

The flashlight fell from my hand. I spun away from the lights in my face.

"She saw too much," one of them said. "Don't let her escape."

I started to run.

OWOOOOOOO. The creature in the trailer howled and heaved himself against its side, making the trailer bounce.

I glanced back to see the two men coming after me. Their lights danced on the ground as they ran.

I ducked my head beneath a low tree branch and dived into a clump of tall weeds. I forced myself to run faster, their angry cries ringing in my ears. So close . . . they were so close behind me.

I can't outrun them, I realized. And I can't see well enough to find a good place to hide.

My feet slid out from under me on a wet patch of mud. I fell hard, landing on my back.

I heard one of the men laugh. The beams from their flashlights swept over me.

I forced myself to my feet. Grabbed a fallen tree branch—and heaved it at them blindly.

I heard it thud to the ground.

The men were silent now, running after me. Closing in.

My side ached. My back throbbed from my fall.

They're going to catch me, I realized. I can't let them. I have to get to Dr. Carpenter. I have to tell her about the pig creature. If I can get to her, maybe we can stop Dad. Together we can stop him.

I scrambled over a low mound of flat stones. Then ducked into a string of tall evergreen trees.

"Where is she?" I heard one of the men ask. "Stop running! We just want to *talk* to you!"

Liar.

I huddled in the dark safety of a broad evergreen tree. But a few seconds later I heard their footsteps crunching closer.

I lowered my head and darted into a wide clearing.

A mistake. A terrible mistake. Now I had nowhere to hide.

"There she is!" I heard one of the men say. "I've got her now."

I saw their lights moving on the other side of the evergreens.

I started to run across the tall grass. But I stumbled over something. Something big and soft.

I bent down to see what it was.

"Ohhhhh." I groaned as I realized I was leaning over the dead deer. The ripped open, half-eaten deer.

The smell of rotting flesh rose up to my nostrils, sickening me.

The torn skin hung loosely over the remaining bones.

I looked up and saw the lights moving. The men were running toward me, pushing their way through the evergreen trees.

In seconds they would see me.

Where could I hide? No trees or rocks or shrubs in the clearing. How could I hide?

I took a deep breath.

I grabbed a flap of the deer's skin. I tugged it up. It felt heavy and wet in my hands.

The sour smell washed over me. I held my breath to keep from puking.

I pulled the skin flap up as far as it would go.

And I climbed inside the deer.

The wet deer skin flapped against my body. As I hunched down, the putrid guts squished against the knees of my jeans. Bones jabbed me in the side.

I pulled the skin tighter around me, but it was slippery and I had trouble gripping it.

Flies buzzed above me. I could feel the moist guts seeping into my clothes.

I shut my eyes and held on tight, covered by the deer skin. The back of my neck itched, but I couldn't scratch it. Something wet and gloppy fell onto my forehead.

I realized I'd been holding my breath the whole time. My chest felt about to burst. I had to breathe. The thick, sour odor made me want to scream. My stomach heaved.

I'm inside a dead deer, I thought. My whole body started to shake. Inside a dead deer . . .

Above me I heard the crunch of footsteps. Voices. "Where is she? How did we lose her?"

"She didn't go far."

I struggled to calm my stomach. I tried not to breathe in the foul smell. But I couldn't hold my breath any longer. I took in a small gulp of air—and threw up.

"Ooooo," I let out a sick moan.

The sound of the footsteps came closer. I felt a hard *thud* and realized one of the men had kicked the deer corpse.

I clamped my mouth shut to keep from crying out.

"This deer looks like it was hit by a truck."

"What a stink. Did you forget your deodorant today?"

They both laughed.

"This deer wasn't killed by a normal animal," I heard one of them say. "Do you think our friend is nearby?"

"I wouldn't be surprised. He sure gets hungry, doesn't he?"

"Well, he *is* a pig! Ha ha!"

"We'll find him soon if he leaves us a trail like this."

I shivered under the disgusting blanket of rancid skin and fur. My whole body itched. My clothes were wet with deer guts. Wet from my own vomit. A new wave of nausea washed over me.

If only they would move on and let me get out of here.

But no. I heard more muttering. Then footsteps. Calls of hello.

Someone else had joined them. I struggled to hear their words. But they had moved farther away.

And then I heard a voice clearly. "Why did you call me?"

I gasped. The deer skin slipped from my hands. I grabbed it back. Struggled to remain silent.

The voice. I recognized it. I recognized it so well. MY DAD.

Should I get up? Should I climb out of the deer corpse and run to my dad? He may be crazy, I thought. But he isn't going to let these men harm his own daughter!

I started to pull back the deer skin, but stopped when Dad spoke. "Why did you call me? What's the problem?" he asked.

"It's your daughter," one of the men said.

"Laura? She was here?"

"She opened the trailer. She saw it. She saw the creature."

"Oh, no," Dad moaned. "Why didn't you stop her?"

"We tried. But she gave us the slip. So we called you."

"She didn't go far," the other man said.

"Well, let's find her!" my dad cried. He sounded very angry. "Get her—before she ruins everything!"

My own dad!

I froze, gripped with horror.

My own dad wanted to catch me now. He really is crazy, I thought. He really is a monster!

I heard their voices fade as they walked away. "Split up," Dad said. "We'll find her by morning."

Then . . . silence.

I didn't move.

I shut my eyes and tried to think.

I couldn't go home. Where could I go?

My own dad . . . My own dad . . .

I had to go somewhere. I had to find help.

I pulled myself slowly out of the deer corpse. My clothes were wet and stained. I tried to wipe the thick, smelly guts off my arms, off my forehead. I pulled a disgusting glob out of my hair.

Up ahead, I heard one of the men cough. I turned away quickly and hurried off in the other direction. My legs felt stiff. My back ached. Every time I breathed, I inhaled that disgusting odor.

Where was I going? I didn't care. I just wanted to get away from those voices. Away from those men. Away from my dad.

I moved as if in a daze, as if wandering through a bad dream. A few minutes later I crept into my backyard. I hadn't even realized I was heading home.

I listened at the shed door. Silent. Then I sneaked all the way around the house, peering into the dark windows.

Dad wasn't home yet. He was still out searching for me.

Feeling shaky and sick, I stepped in through the back door and hurried to my room.

"This is my house," I said out loud. "My house."

But I was no longer safe here. Because I lived with an enemy. I lived with a *monster*!

I tore off the disgusting clothes and shoved them into my closet. Then I took a fast shower, listening hard, praying my dad wouldn't return.

The warm water felt so wonderful. I wanted to shower for hours and shampoo my hair a dozen times. But I knew I had to get out of there fast.

I pulled on fresh jeans and a sweatshirt and ran out through the front door. I expected the night darkness to hide me. But the sky was a pink-gray now. Almost morning.

I headed straight for the animal hospital.

I walked silently through the woods, alert,

looking . . . listening for Dad and the men.

The morning dew made the ground soft and muddy. The pink morning sunlight sent down shimmering patches of color.

"Oh." I stopped when I heard the rustle of bushes. Saw them shaking. I wasn't alone.

I ducked behind a tree—and gasped with relief when I saw Joe. I ran from my hiding place. Ran up to him and almost hugged him!

"Joe!" A startled laugh escaped my throat. "What are you doing up so early?"

He stopped a few feet from me. "Oh—Laura. Hi! What are *you* doing here?"

"It's—it's kind of a long story," I said. I kept glancing around nervously, afraid my dad would appear at any moment.

"I—I've been up all night," I told Joe.

"Why?" Joe asked. "Are you okay?"

"I need help," I said. "Will you help me get to the animal hospital? Some men are trying to catch me and—"

I reached up. He had something green stuck in his hair. A caterpillar. I grabbed it.

"NO!" Joe screamed. To my shock, he jerked away from me—

—and his hair came off in my hand!

"OHH!" we both cried out at once.

I stared at the long, shiny black hair in my hand. A wig!

I turned back to Joe. His eyes were bulging with horror.

And his head—his head was entirely bald.

With two pointed, pink PIG EARS at the top!

No!" I gasped.

Joe's mouth dropped open—and I saw his teeth—two rows of them. One was normal . . . human, the other was a set of pointed pig teeth.

"I'm sorry—" Joe whispered. "I didn't want you to know."

"I . . . don't understand," I choked out.

Joe's expression turned angry. "You'll understand soon enough!" he cried. "I'm the creature, Laura. I'm the creature that's been upsetting all the animals in the woods. Because I'm not normal."

He let out an angry cry. "I'm a *creature*! The bats, the dogs, the birds—they've been acting strange because of me. Because I'm a freak. Because they know I don't belong!"

"But—" I struggled to form words. I couldn't think straight. I couldn't take my eyes off his round, bald head, his pig ears.

"And sometimes . . . sometimes I get so hungry," Joe said, clenching his pointed teeth. "I do terrible things. I'm sorry, Laura. Really sorry."

"The deer?" I gasped. "It was you who chewed up the deer? And attacked Georgie? And . . . and that was *your* hut with all the animal bones and heads?"

He didn't answer. He snatched the wig from my hand. "I . . . I came to the woods. I just wanted some fresh air," he said, his voice trembling. "I just wanted to live free for a while. I'm so tired of being locked up . . . hidden away . . . a prisoner."

Then Joe spun away, breathing hard, grunting like an animal—and ran off.

I stood frozen, watching him vanish into the trees. I hugged myself, thinking hard. Trying to make sense of everything.

How did he become a creature like that? Did Dad do that to him?

Was my dad experimenting on humans, too?

I felt sick. Dizzy.

"Dr. Carpenter." I uttered her name out loud. I needed Dr. Carpenter to help me sort this all out.

The sun was still low over the trees as I pulled open the front door to the animal hospital. The reception room was dark. No one behind the desk.

I glanced at the wall clock. Only seven-thirty. Most of the staff wouldn't be here this early.

I heard the whimper of animals down the long hall. A cat cried. It sounded so human—like a baby.

"Is anyone here?" I shouted. "Dr. Carpenter? It's me—Laura!"

No reply.

Maybe she's in one of the research labs, I thought. I knew she sometimes came in early before the patients started arriving.

I started down the long hall toward the lab. Only a few of the ceiling lights were on. The endless hall with its faded walls, closed doors, and long shadows seemed creepy in the dim light. The old floors creaked under my feet. Animals whimpered and howled.

"Is—is anyone here?" I called. "Dr. Carpenter?"

I pulled open a door. I thought it led to a lab. But it was filled with animal cages and cartons of pet food.

I stopped when I thought I heard footsteps. "Dr. Carpenter?"

No. The sounds vanished. A dog barked. The floor creaked.

I turned a corner into another long hall of doors. "Hello!" I called. "Anyone?"

I pulled open another door. An empty lab.

I knew the research lab was somewhere here in the back. But which door?

I tried the next door. A shrill howl greeted me. Other animals cried out in the darkness. Cages rattled and shook.

I clicked on the light—and gasped. "No!"

I stood frozen in the doorway, gaping at the cages that lined the back of the lab. A wall of cages with animals inside . . . not animals . . .

Creatures.

Ugly creatures. All of them. Poodles with pointed pig ears, cats with pig snouts, monkeys, furless monkeys, covered in pink pigskin.

But the worst, the most hideous, were the creatures in the tall cages. Pigs with *human* bodies, *human* arms and legs. Pigs the size of children, standing on two legs. Pigs with long, dark human hair growing out of their heads.

The pig creatures grabbed the bars of their cages with human hands.

No. Some of them had *pig hooves* at the ends of their arms.

I stepped inside the room and stared at a creature with a short, stubby pig body—and long, brown hair falling over its face. A pig face—with human lips!

They opened their snouts wide and grunted and cried. They banged hooves against the cage bars.

I wandered closer as if hypnotized. What were these creatures? Why were they here?

A giant pig with human legs and arms and human ears banged its head against the bars, too big for its cage. Beside it I saw a tiny pig creature. A pig *with a long, horse tail!*

The tiny creature was sick on its side, lying in a

puddle of yellow vomit. I bent down to see him better—

And felt a strong hand grab my hair.

The giant pig creature!

Grunting loudly, he shoved his arms through the cage bars—and grabbed my head with two hands.

Unnnh . . . unnnh . . . unnnnh . . .

He rubbed his hot, wet hands over my face. Then lowered them to my neck—and began to squeeze.

"Unnnh." I let out a choked groan. I struggled to pry the big hands off me.

But the creature was too strong. He pulled me up against the cage. His breath stank. His hands tightened around my throat.

The animals were bleating and crying, shaking their cages, jumping up and down. So loud . . . so loud my ears rang.

But as my breath was choked off, the sounds began to fade. The lights began to dim.

Just as my body started to sag, I heard a shout.

And then another angry shout. And the big hands slid off my neck. The grunting creature pulled its arms back into the cage.

I could breathe again. Rubbing my aching throat, I sucked in breath after breath.

And then I turned and saw Dr. Carpenter hurrying across the room. Her face twisted in shock. "What are you doing here?"

She didn't wait for me to answer. She put an arm around my shoulder tenderly and examined my neck. "Are you okay, dear? Can you breathe? That big guy can be dangerous."

"I . . . I . . . " My throat ached so badly, I could barely whisper. "Those creatures . . . " I finally said, waving my hand to the cages. "Did my dad make them all?"

Dr. Carpenter narrowed her eyes at me. "You shouldn't be here, Laura."

"But—but—" I sputtered.

"You should have listened to him," Dr. Carpenter said. "You should have stayed out of the woods."

She sighed. "And now he'll be coming here after you, won't he? He'll be coming to stop my work. He already rounded up some of the creatures that escaped from my lab. He's been scouting the woods, searching for them."

"I—I don't understand!" I cried. "Please—"

"Well . . . I can't let him stop me," Dr. Carpenter said angrily. "Not until I've found a cure."

I blinked. "A cure?" I asked. "A cure for what?"

She didn't seem to hear me. Her eyes were on the cages now. "These poor creatures are all failures," she said, shaking her head. "Look at them. Look what I've done to them. Poor things . . . But I have to succeed. I have to."

She turned back to me, her green eyes glowing. "Maybe you can help, Laura."

I felt a chill roll down my back. "Huh? Me?"

She grabbed my shoulder and brought her face close to mine. "You wouldn't mind sacrificing, would you? Would you, Laura? If it would save a life?"

"S-sacrifice?"

I realized I was trembling in terror. What was Dr. Carpenter saying? I couldn't understand her.

"Are these my dad's creatures?" I asked. "Are you trying to cure them? Are you going to make them normal again?"

Dr. Carpenter took a step back from me. She studied my face for a moment, then shook her head. "No, Laura. They're not your father's creatures. They're mine."

"Yours?" my voice shook. "What do you mean?"

"You'll understand soon." She took my arm. "I've been preparing you," she said. "That shot I gave you—it wasn't for your neck wound. The shot was to prepare you . . . for the gene transfer."

"Noooo!" I let out a scream and tore free from her grasp.

Then I spun away and lurched for the door.

Pounding their cages, the creatures began to bleat and howl. I glanced back and saw Dr. Carpenter chasing after me.

"OWWWW!" I cried out as I ran into a tall cage by the door. The cage clattered onto its side. And dozens of bats flapped out, chittering and whistling.

The bats swooped up to the ceiling, then down,

fluttering back and forth across the lab.

As Dr. Carpenter struggled with them, I ducked out the door. Into the long, dark hall.

My shoes pounded on the faded rug, the floor creaking and squeaking as I ran. I could still hear the flapping of the bats—and Dr. Carpenter's shrill cries as she came after me.

Panting hard, I wheeled around a corner—and ran into somebody.

"Oh—!" A hard collision. I caught my balance quickly.

And stared at Joe. He had put his black wig back on. He gaped at me in shock.

"Huh? You're here?" I cried. "You've got to help me, Joe! Help me get away from her! She's crazy!"

To my surprise, Joe grabbed me around the waist. And pushed me against the wall.

"I've got her!" he shouted. "Here she is! I've got her, Mom!"

"Huh? What are you *saying*, Joe?" I shrieked.

Joe didn't answer me. He kept me pinned against the wall. I struggled against him. Struggled to push free. But I wasn't strong enough.

Dr. Carpenter hurried up to us. "Good," she muttered. They grabbed my arms and pulled me into another lab. Then they shoved me into a tall cage. Dr. Carpenter slammed the cage door shut and locked it.

I turned and saw two ugly pig creatures behind me in the cage. One had long, blond hair with a pig face covered with brown speckles. The other one had sharp, black horns sprouting from its pig head. It looked as if it were the combination of a pig and a ram.

"Please—let me out!" I wailed. "Please—!"

The speckled pig creature lurched forward and poked me in the side with a sharp hoof.

My heart pounded as the other one raised furry paws and ran one through my hair as if brushing it.

"Please—let me out."

The horned creature brought its face close to mine. It bared its teeth—as sharp as razors.

"It's—it's going to bite me." I backed away from the beast. Pressed myself into a corner of the cage. "Please—let me out."

"I'm sorry, Laura," she said. "But we can't have you running away again. We need you too badly."

"Need me? For what?" My voice came out high and shrill.

Bats fluttered in and out of the room. I gazed frantically around the lab. Cages were stacked high along the back wall. The cages were filled with squealing pigs.

In the center of the room stood a wall of electronic equipment. I saw three or four computer monitors. Several blinking control panels. Two metal cones were attached at either end. On a shiny metal table, syringes gleamed under the lab lights.

The pig creature with the horns grunted at me, baring its pointed teeth, licking its snout with a long pink tongue. The other one swiped at me with its hoof.

"You can't keep me here!" I cried. I charged at the bars and gripped the door, struggling to shove it open. It wouldn't budge.

"It won't take long," Dr. Carpenter replied. "It will all be over by the time your dad comes looking for you."

She was pushing buttons and spinning dials on the control panel. "Joe, bring down that pig on top. Cage number forty."

Joe hurried to obey. He opened the cage and lifted out a small pink-and-white pig. Holding it tightly in both hands, he carried it to Dr. Carpenter. She lifted the pig's head into one of the metal cones and began strapping it in.

Lights flashed on the control panel.

Two bats swooped into the lab, then soared back out.

"You lied to me!" I screamed. "You said my dad was doing the cruel experiments."

"I had to lie. I had no choice," Dr. Carpenter said. "Four years ago, right before we moved here, I found a way to change genes using electric shock. I was so close to creating a gene that could fight off viruses. So close. But then we had the terrible accident."

She turned and gazed at Joe. He had finished strapping the pig under the cone. Now he held the pig's leg while Dr. Carpenter inserted a syringe filled with a yellow liquid. The pig let out a sharp squeal as the needle penetrated its skin.

"During one of the cell transfers, Joe pricked himself with a syringe filled with pig cells. He stumbled back in surprise—stumbled directly into the path of the electric current," Dr. Carpenter continued. "His cells combined with pig cells."

She patted his cheek. "My poor little boy . . . he . . .

he hasn't been the same. He . . . " Tears formed in her eyes.

"We moved here so I'd have a safe place to live," Joe said. "No one would ask about me here. No one knew me here. And Mom could continue her research. To change me back."

"Joe, I—I—thought you were my friend," I stammered.

"I don't have friends anymore, Laura," he said softly. "I have to hide in the house most of the time. Until the hunger starts. That deep hunger for fresh meat. Then I have to hunt the woods. . . ." His voice trailed off.

"Joe," Dr. Carpenter sobbed. "I'm sorry. So sorry."

"You'll change me back, Mom," Joe said soothingly. "I know you will."

Dr. Carpenter turned to me. "I've been spending all my time trying to find a way to reverse the process. That's what all these animals are for. To help me change Joe back to normal."

"But, my dad—" I started.

"Your dad didn't approve of my experiments. He didn't know about Joe. I kept him hidden. But he didn't approve of the way I was treating the animals. He said I was going against the laws of nature. He tried to make me stop. The animals were dying. But I couldn't stop. I found that if I dissected them, I could learn what went wrong. I had to kill more—until I found the cure."

If we kill them, we can learn more. How many can we kill? The words from the binder in Dad's shed exploded in my mind. "Those were *your* notes in the shed!" I gasped.

My heart sank. I should have trusted my father. He'd never hurt an animal. I should have believed in him. My dad could never hurt a living thing.

Dr. Carpenter turned to Joe. "Enough talk. We haven't much time. Help me get Laura hooked up to the other transfer cone. Then we'll inject her."

"No!" I screamed, pushing away the two pig creatures. "No! Please!"

"I haven't had a human to experiment on in some time," Dr. Carpenter said, unlocking the cage door. "But now you're here. Wouldn't you like to be the one who helps me turn Joe back to normal?"

"No!" I screamed. "Please! Please!"

She grabbed me with both hands and tugged me from the cage. Then she shoved me under the metal cone.

I tried to kick free. But she was too strong. She pinned me against the side of the machine. And pulled the cone down over my hair.

"Wait, Mom—don't!" Joe screamed. "I don't like this. I can't go through with it! Laura is my friend!"

"She's not your friend!" Dr. Carpenter snapped. She tightened a strap under my chin to hold me under the cone. "Don't you understand? Her father will destroy me before I cure you!"

"Mom—" Joe cried.

Dr. Carpenter turned to me. "The current will shoot between the two cones," she explained. "It doesn't hurt, Laura. Not at all. We'll inject you with something to help the pig's cells bind to yours. And this machine will take care of the rest. You won't even feel it."

"Noooo! Noooo! Please!" I struggled to free myself.

But I had no time.

She grabbed a syringe—and jabbed it into my arm. I screamed as the pain throbbed up my arm.

She pulled the needle out quickly, scratching herself. She blotted the blood with her lab coat. Then she reached past me to the control panel. Clutched a long handle. And threw the switch.

I heard the crackle of electricity.

I saw Joe grab his mother around the waist and try to pull her away.

As they wrestled, the lab door swung open behind them.

"Dad!" I screamed. "Help me!"

An electrical current jolted between the two metal cones. The pig on the other side squealed and began to kick its feet.

A bat swooped into the room. It flew low over my dad, heading right for the electrical current.

Dr. Carpenter turned to face my dad. "Get out of here!" she screamed, backing away from him. "You've done enough!"

Dad kept coming, his eyes narrowed angrily on her, his fists knotted at his sides.

The bat swooped past my head.

Dr. Carpenter took another step back. "You can't

stop me!" she screamed at my father. "You can't! I'm warning you—"

But he didn't stop. He came after her. Step by step. His hands clamped into fists.

Backing her up . . . Backing her up . . .

And then she let out a high shriek as she stumbled—and fell back—into the electrical current.

I screamed, too, as I saw the bat swoop into the stream of electricity.

ZZZAAAAAP.

The whole room sizzled and crackled.

I saw Dr. Carpenter and the bat outlined in bright yellow.

I saw the bat explode in the crackling current. Its guts sprayed Dr. Carpenter as she shrieked in terror.

And then I shut my eyes. It was too horrible. Too ugly.

Too terrifying.

I didn't open my eyes until I felt the metal cone being lifted off my head. Dad pulled me out into the hall.

He hugged me tightly. I gazed up at him, still dazed.

"It's okay now, Laura," Dad said softly. "It's all over. My work is done. We've stopped her. I've been gathering evidence. Working so hard."

"But, Dad—" I choked out. "The creatures in the shed. The binder you stole from her . . . "

"I tried to stop her research. I knew her experiments were wrong," he said. "That's why she fired me. But I took her notes. I've been trying to cure the animals she changed."

He guided me gently down the hall and led me out of the building. "Where are they?" I asked, glancing back at the animal hospital. "Where are Joe and Dr. Carpenter?"

"They ran while I was freeing you. But don't

worry. They won't get far. We'll find them."

Dad and I were home a few minutes later. I followed him into the kitchen.

He picked up an envelope from the kitchen counter and ripped it in half.

"What's that?" I asked.

"Your plane ticket to Chicago." He tossed the pieces into the trash. "I never wanted to send you away," he said. "But I was so scared. I knew how vicious those creatures could be. I only wanted to protect you."

He shook his head. "In the woods last night you shouldn't have run. I only wanted to protect you, Laura."

I rushed forward to hug him. We hugged for a long time.

Then my eyes drifted to the kitchen window. I gazed into the woods. I thought about Joe. Would I ever see him again? I wondered.

And would the woods return to normal now?

Would *anything* ever be normal again?

That night I was so tired. But I couldn't fall asleep.

I lay in bed, staring at the pale half-moon outside my window. It looked like a smile. A grin in the dark.

I had finally started to drift off. My eyes were just closing—when I heard a fluttering sound.

Something flapping against the window glass.

I sat up, alert.

What *was* that? A bat?

Yes. A bat floating outside the window, beating its wings against the glass.

"Huh?" I crept out of bed. I made my way to the window.

Thump thump.

The wings bumped and scraped the glass as the bat hovered at the window.

I crept closer. Watching the flapping wings. The tiny, round body. The bat claws . . .

And the face . . .

The face . . .

Dr. Carpenter's face on the bat's body!

Flapping, bumping against the window, she stared in at me. Her face tiny now, where the bat's head should be. Her green eyes wide with horror.

And then she opened her mouth wide.

Staring at each other through the glass, we both opened our mouths—and screamed and screamed and screamed.

ABOUT THE AUTHOR

R.L. STINE says he has a great job. "My job is to give kids the CREEPS!" With his scary books, R.L. has terrified kids all over the world. He has sold over 300 million books, making him the best-selling children's author in history.

These days, R.L. is dishing out new frights in his series THE NIGHTMARE ROOM. When he isn't working, he likes to read old mysteries, watch *SpongeBob Squarepants* on TV, and take his dog, Nadine, for long walks around New York City, where he lives with his wife, Jane, and son, Matthew.

"I love taking my readers to scary places," R.L. says. "Do you know the scariest place of all? It's your MIND!"

Take a look at what's ahead in
THE NIGHTMARE ROOM #7
The Howler

Another eerie howl floated into the room. Then, more scratching sounds.

"Scott—let the cat in!" Scott's mom called from the other room. "She's at the back door again. Don't you hear her?"

"I'll get her, Mom," Scott called. He trotted to the door. "Dumb cat," he muttered.

I let out a long sigh.

Vanessa laughed. "Did you think you heard a ghost?"

"No," I lied. "I knew it was a cat." I could feel my face growing hot. I always blush whenever I tell a lie.

I felt a little shaky. Why did I suddenly think that Scott really had ghosts in his house?

I guess it was because I wanted to believe *so much*.

Matilda, Scott's black cat, came running over our feet, desperate to get to her water dish. Scott appeared in the kitchen doorway. "Come on. We don't want to keep the ghosts waiting."

We followed him through the front hall to the stairs. The hall was long and dark, with ghostly gray wallpaper and lights on the walls shaped like candles.

"Scott—who is here?" his mother shouted from the living room.

"It's Spencer and Vanessa," he called to her. And then he added in a deep voice that was supposed to be scary, "They've come to visit the Haunted Mansion."

"Huh?" his mother called. "Haunted *what*?"

"She tries to keep the ghosts a secret," Scott whispered to us. "She doesn't want anyone to know about them."

"Yeah. Sure," I muttered.

The wooden stairs creaked and groaned as Vanessa and I followed him upstairs. "Sometimes, I hear footsteps going up and down these stairs late at night," Scott said. "I flash on the lights—and there's no one here."

Vanessa shook her head. "He's good," she whispered. "He's real good. He almost has *me* believing!"

"Not me," I whispered back.

In the upstairs hall, we stopped under a door in the ceiling. Scott grabbed a rope that hung down from the door.

"This leads to the attic," he said. "I think this is where the ghosts hang out before dark."

He tugged the rope. The door creaked down. There were wooden stairs built on the other side of the door. "Careful. Some of these stairs are rotted," Scott warned.

I started up the stairs, slowly, one at a time. The

stairs were steep, and there was nothing to hold on to.

Halfway up, I turned back to Scott. "You're telling us we'll see ghosts up here?"

He nodded solemnly. "They're not shy. They're not afraid of us. They don't care if we see them or not."

I climbed the rest of the way and waited for Vanessa and Scott to join me. The attic was long and low-ceilinged. It was one big, L-shaped room that curved off to the right.

There was only one window, smeared with a thick layer of dust. Orange sunlight seeped through, but it lit just a small part of the room. The rest of the attic lay in shadow.

I blinked several times, waiting for my eyes to adjust to the strange light. The attic was cluttered with cartons, and stacks of magazines, books, and furniture. I saw couches and chairs covered in sheets, like Halloween ghosts.

Cobwebs clung to an old coat rack, tilted against one wall. A stack of framed photographs leaned against the opposite wall. The photos were dark, the paper yellowed and cracked.

In one of the photos, a strange-looking boy in a black cap appeared to stare out at us. He had dark circles around his sad eyes. His face was puckered like a prune. He looked more like a monkey than a boy.

"Is that your baby picture?" Vanessa joked to Scott.

He raised a finger to his lips. "Ssshhhh. Do you want to see a ghost or not?"

We stepped out of the light, into the shadowy area of the room. My shoes slid on the thick layer of dust over the floor. I tripped over a small table, but caught it before it fell.

We turned the corner. I squinted to see. This section of the attic was totally dark.

Scott pulled a light cord. A tiny ceiling bulb flickered on.

In the dim light, I saw an old rocking chair with one arm broken. A wooden clock standing on its side. A stack of dishes.

And then . . .

And then . . .

Vanessa and I saw her at the same time. An old woman—so pale, her face so ghostly pale—standing against the curtained back wall. Her old-fashioned clothes were faded. No color. No color anywhere.

My mouth dropped open. A tiny cry burst out.

Vanessa grabbed my hand. "Scott wasn't kidding!" she whispered.